one

. . .

Brady

Six Months Prior...

I roll over and drape my arm across the slim waist of the gorgeous woman next to me. The woman who rocked my fucking world last night.

I'm no stranger to one-night stands. In fact, I have rules to ensure all my hookups remain just that, which is why I'm waking in a high-end hotel room this morning.

My five-year-old son, Theo, stayed with his mom, Hannah, overnight, but regardless, women don't come back to my place. The last thing I need in my life is a psycho jersey chaser knowing where I live and showing up unannounced. It's Hooking Up 101 for the best wide receiver for the San Francisco Kingsmen.

I pull her toward me and my morning wood pokes into her ass. She stirs in her sleep and rolls over to face me. She blinks a few times before fully opening her dark, alluring eyes, focusing on me. Once opened, she widens her eyes and gasps, bolting upright in bed.

The sheet slides to her waist, gifting me the perfect view

of her modest but perky breasts. Her eyes follow mine and she snags the sheet, yanking it to her neck.

I'm not sure why she's being modest. Last night I had her bending every which way. She's gotta be a gymnast.

I chuckle and flop on my back. "Good morning."

I link my hands behind my head and my elbows fall to the sides. She left me enough sheet for my lower half to be covered, but her gaze roams down my chiseled chest to the tented sheet caused by my dick. She licks her bottom lip and my cock twitches, hoping that means we'll go another round.

"Morning," she says in a soft voice.

At the club last night, with all the music, we had to shout to hear each other. It wasn't until we got to the hotel that I fell in love with her voice. It's soft and alluring and comforting. Maybe she's a nurse or something where she needs a good bedside manner.

I reach to touch her thick, wavy dark hair hanging over one shoulder, but she shuffles away. "I should probably get going."

My forehead creases. She looks at the tent, licks her lips, and her cheeks are flushed. She wants me to convince her. "Do you have to run off so quick?"

Most one-night stands, I would have been long gone by now. Most one-night stands, I'd have left them the room service menu and a classic "had a great time" note by now. Most one-night stands, I don't lazily wake up naked under a sheet, hoping for another round. But this petite spitfire has something the others didn't. I just can't pinpoint what it is.

"I need to get home." Her eyes skim the area, searching for her clothes strewn around the room, and return to me. We weren't exactly careful when undressing last night. The best sign of a one-night stand. "Can you turn around or close your eyes or something?"

I bark out a laugh. "Sweetie, I've already seen everything. And hell, I've already tasted everything too."

Her cheeks pinken and my heart warms from garnering that reaction from her.

"Even so, do you mind?" Her eyes widen, a tone of annoyance in her words.

"I gotta hit the head anyway." I whip the sheet off and stand, then strut across the large suite to the bathroom, feeling her gaze on my bare ass every inch of the way.

Oh yeah, she wants me as badly as I want her again. She just doesn't want to admit it for some reason.

I finish my business and return to the suite. She sits in the chair snuggled in the corner, buckling the ankle strap of her heel, dressed in the outfit she wore last night—a long see-through lace skirt with booty shorts underneath, a white V-neck crop, and a bright-pink jacket that ends at her waist.

While most of the other women at the club were wearing short, skintight dresses, this woman had a style all her own. It was the first thing I noticed about her and I liked that she wasn't afraid to stand out in a crowd. It's refreshing actually.

She rises from the chair and looks at me expectantly. "Think everyone in the lobby will know I'm doing the walk of shame?" Her laugh sounds empty.

"If they were present last night, they'd know there's nothing shameful about it. In fact, I think we should have a do-over." I draw her into my arms, but she places her hands on my chest to keep our bodies from being flush together.

"You're naked."

I glance down between our bodies at my erection. "You could be too. I asked for a late checkout when we got here last night."

She's shaking her head before I finish talking. "I had a great time, but like you said last night—this isn't going anywhere. We had our fun and now I need to go."

I frown, not liking my own words being recited back to me. "Maybe I spoke too hastily."

"No, you were right." She steps back from me and picks

up her purse from a nearby chair. "It was fun… a lot of fun." Her gaze drags down my naked body again and she clears her throat. "But I'm not looking to get involved with anyone either."

She makes her way to the door and I follow her.

"Let me at least give you my number. Maybe we can meet up again sometime?" I shake my head, not understanding why I want to see her a second time, but the urge isn't one I can control at the moment.

She turns when she's at the door. "No, thanks."

I'm slammed by her response because, in all the years, no one has ever turned me down. I stand there silently.

She giggles, obviously satisfied with herself. "Don't take it personally." She turns back around and grabs the door handle, twisting.

"Wait!"

She looks over her shoulder.

"At least tell me your name."

Last night she said she wanted to keep names out of it. I didn't have to tell her mine—if she didn't recognize me, there were enough people using my first name. But no matter what I tried, she wouldn't budge on hers. At the time, I didn't mind. I'll use whatever pet name when I'm between her legs —sweetie, sexy, babe—it doesn't matter to me. But how the hell do I track her down again if I don't have at least a first name?

"I told you last night. I don't do names." And with her closing the subject, she walks out of the hotel room without a backward glance.

I stand and wait a few beats, thinking maybe she'll change her mind. Even after I shut the door, I anticipate a knock on the door that never comes.

two

. . .

Brady

The doorbell rings and Theo sprints past me, out of his room and down the stairs.

"Slow down! Hold on to the banister!" I shout and follow.

"*Mom!*" he screams.

I've only had him for two days, and Hannah is here to pick him up.

Theo is fussing with the lock on the door by the time I get to the foyer.

"Let me." I reach past him and turn the dead bolt and the lock on the handle, then he twists the doorknob and opens the door.

Theo's shoulders drop when he sees my parents, not his mom.

"Hey, what gives? Is that the kind of welcome I get now?" my mom says.

Theo gives her a smile. "I thought you were Mom. Sorry, Glamma."

Yes, Glamma, not Grandma. Lennon—who is actually my stepmom, but I only think of her as my mom—insists that she's too cool, too young, and too progressive to ever be called Grandma. And she's right. I often wonder how a stuffy investment banker like my dad scored a woman who owns a sex toy company.

"Make it up to me with a hug," she says, and Theo rushes over and squeezes her legs. Lennon bends over and kisses the top of his head.

When Theo pulls away, he goes straight to my dad and does the same. "Hi, Gramps."

My dad musses his hair. "Hey, champ. You headed back to your mom's house so soon?"

He pulls away and nods vigorously. "Yup. She's taking me to the aquarium today."

My dad smiles. "Very cool."

"I've been there before with my dad. It's so cool. You should see this one fish they have…"

Theo keeps talking as I motion for them to come in. My dad bends and picks Theo up and heads into the family room, intently listening the entire time. Lennon gives my hand a squeeze as she walks past me.

She knows how much sharing custody hurts me. The fact he has to be shuffled back and forth is not what I had in mind. But Hannah and I are better off as co-parents and friends. In the end, I have to believe that our relationship will benefit my son more than if he had two parents who lived in the same house but were unhappy.

The four of us hang out in the family room and Theo shows my parents the latest Lego firetruck he's been working on.

After a while, my dad and Lennon share a look and Lennon stands from the couch and walks over to Theo. "Hey, why don't you show me the new Lego sets you've finished in your room?"

Whenever we finish a Lego set, we place it on display on one of the shelves in his room. While I'm sure Lennon has a mild interest in seeing what he's been working on. I get the impression it's a ruse to get my dad and me alone.

"Oh yeah, Glamma, I almost have the entire city. Dad said next are the boats." He takes her hand and drags her out of the room.

Soon we hear Lennon and Theo's feet on the stairs, him talking nonstop about the one Uncle Chase had to put together because Daddy's friends knocked it over. The kid must have been spying because Chase did an incredible job on that one.

Getting that out of my head, I turn to my dad on the other end of the couch. "Good news or bad news?"

He chuckles. "We never can put one past you."

"You'd always try though. So—good or bad?" A million scary things go through my head. Are they divorcing? No, they seem happy. Something with my brother and sister? Yeah, but they wouldn't drive all the way over here. No way is Lennon pregnant again.

They used to try—a lot. I remember when I was twelve, and they'd pretend my dad was helping Lennon find something in the garage when in reality, they were making out or messing around. One day I called them out on it. Or when Lennon missed putting some presents under the tree on Christmas morning and I found the bag in the garage a couple of weeks later, grabbing my scooter, she tried to tell me that Santa ate too many cookies, and he must've forgotten the presents go under the tree.

"Well… we're hoping you'll think it's good news." My dad has his serious face on. The one I'm used to seeing when he's working on a deal.

"I'm listening."

"Lennon and I are entering negotiations to purchase the Kingsmen. If all goes smoothly, we'll be the owners by the time training camp starts."

I blink and I blink again until my eyes remain wide open. I don't know what I expected my dad to say, but it wasn't that. "Wow. Congratulations, I guess?"

He stares at me, trying to judge my reaction. "Are you okay with this?"

I think about what my parents owning my team means for me and how it might change the way my teammates view me. "I guess… this means you guys will be my bosses." I cringe.

My dad sighs. "Technically, yes, but you'll get no special treatment from us, and we won't interfere with whatever you're doing on the field unless things really go to shit."

I chuckle. "Thanks for the vote of confidence."

"Truth is, we've been looking at buying the team for a while. You being transferred here last year was surprising, causing Lennon and I to table the conversation. We didn't want to interfere in your life. Then we got word Giles Hanover is still looking to sell, but we would never put pen to paper without talking to you first."

I lean back on the couch, hands behind my head. "I appreciate it, Dad, but I wouldn't stand in your way even if I wasn't cool with it. You guys have done so much for me and Theo over the years—"

My dad quickly interrupts me. "That's what parents do, Brady. You know that now yourself."

He's right. There's nothing I wouldn't do for my little boy. I myself never wanted for anything growing up.

I nod. "I know. I guess I'm saying if you want to do this, you should. Realistically, I'm thirty-two. My days of playing football are numbered, whereas you could own the team for decades if you wanted. I won't stand in the way of that."

My dad stands and clamps me on the shoulder. "All right then. Wish us luck. Giles Hanover is a class A prick I don't trust with an ounce of my life." Then he grows serious. "Needless to say, you cannot tell anyone about this."

"My lips are sealed." The sound of footsteps pounding on the stairs causes me to call out, "Use the banister!"

My dad smirks. "He reminds me a lot of you."

"So, I was a complete handful at his age?"

Theo and Mom join us in the family room.

"Dad! Glamma said she'll take me to Legoland if I'm good for Mom this weekend." His eyes are wide and full of excitement as he bounces up and down in front of me.

"Isn't that near San Diego?" I ask, looking at my mom.

She waves me off. "We'll take the jet down and make a day of it."

I'm not gonna lie and say it's not nice to have money at your disposal, and my parents have always had money, that's for sure. But it wasn't until I was a teenager that they joined the one-percent club. I don't want Theo to grow up thinking it's normal to jump on a private plane for a day trip.

"Mom…"

She holds up both hands. "What? I'm not allowed to spoil my only grandchild?"

She's saved from my answer when the doorbell rings and Theo runs out of the room.

"We should get going anyway," my dad says.

My mom looks between us. "You two spoke?"

"All's good," Dad says.

She gives me a hug. "Promise we won't cramp your style."

I laugh and pull away. "I'm more worried about the opposite really."

She swats me on the arm and gives me a wink.

Growing up with a mom like her required being confident I could kick every kid's butt at my school. When your mother owns a sex toy company, has tatted up her arms, and gives zero fucks what anyone else thinks, it's hard walking in on day one of school or having her as a trip chaperone. Although everyone got to know her and loved her because she was awesome, it was hard during those adolescent years when all I wanted to do was blend in with everyone.

Then there's the whole thing that no subject is taboo or off the table. Picture your mom giving you sex tips after she finds you having sex with a girl. And I'm not talking the usual "wear a condom" stuff either. More like an introduction to where to find the G-spot and how to ease a woman into anal sex so you make her quiver.

We follow Theo to the front door where he's once again messing with the lock. The exact reason I installed a latch on top that only I can reach. I lean in over him, unlock the door, and swing it open.

"Mommy!" He jumps into Hannah.

She fumbles with her bag but grabs him at the last minute, enveloping him in a hug. She smiles at me over his shoulder, then notices my parents standing behind me when she straightens and puts Theo on her hip. "Hi, Lennon, hi, Jasper."

"Hey, Hannah. We were just leaving." My dad slides around the side of me.

My parents give her a quick hug as they step onto the porch.

Amazing how we can be so civil. We're all on good terms. There was never any drama between Hannah and me when things didn't work out. The two of us were meant to be a hookup, but when she got pregnant, we tried to make a relationship of it.

Before my dad married Lennon, I lived in a one-parent-absent household and hated it. I wanted more than anything to be able to give Theo the traditional nuclear family. But it became obvious pretty quickly that Hannah and I were better as friends and co-parents than lovers. So we made the mutual decision to split before things took a turn and we ended up resenting or hating one another. Our relationship has been smooth as glass since.

I say goodbye to my parents, as does Theo, and we turn to Hannah. "He's pretty much ready. There's just a couple of things he still has to pack."

Hannah runs her hands through Theo's dark strands.

"Hey, buddy, why don't you go finish packing while I talk to your dad for a minute, okay?"

I'm familiar with the look on her face and the tone of her voice, causing my stomach to tighten. She's about to change the good thing we have going here. I knew it was too good to be true when she agreed to move to San Francisco when I took the trade last year.

Or maybe she's met someone. We have the condition that Theo doesn't get introduced unless it's serious. I have no idea how I'd handle a new man in her life. I mean, I know it's inevitable. Truth be told, I'm surprised it hasn't happened yet. Hannah is attractive with her long blonde hair, blue eyes, and fit body.

Theo rushes off upstairs, and I gesture in the direction of the family room. "Come on in." She sits on the couch and I sit in the chair, my forearms resting on my knees, my hands clasped together. "Everything okay?"

She nods and presses her lips together, a sure sign that she's nervous to talk to me about whatever this is. "I wanted to talk to you about something without Theo here because I didn't know how you'd feel about it."

Definitely a new man. "Okay… what's up?" I shift on the chair, cracking my neck side to side.

She blows out a breath. I glance at her left hand. No ring.

"I got a call about an opportunity to go overseas for work. My boss wants me to head up our team's response to the crisis in eastern Europe."

Elation hits me, and I spring up from the chair. "That's awesome, Han. Congrats!" I grab her and hug her.

She sighs and nods, lightly patting my back before drawing back from the contact. "The thing is that this contract would likely be for a few months, not a few days or weeks. Months."

"Oh." I lean back and bite my inner cheek. "When would you be leaving?"

Piper Rayne

She clasps her hands in her lap. "Within the next couple of weeks."

"Is it safe where you're going?" That's of paramount importance to me. I've seen what's going on over there in the news and I don't want my child's mother in the middle of it. I don't want my child without a mother.

She nods. "I wouldn't go otherwise, but yes. I'll be far from the conflict."

My brain quickly runs through the timing. If she's gone for months, her absence will run into training camp and football season, a time when she would normally stay close to home because of how long my days are.

"Shit, Han, training camp is coming up." I run a hand down my face.

Hannah cringes. "I know. I thought maybe… you could use a live-in nanny while I'm gone." Something must cross my face because she quickly backtracks. "If you don't like the idea, I can just decline the opportunity. It's not the end of the world. I'm sure others will come up."

Guilt tugs in my gut. She's spent the last six years at the mercy of my career and never once complained. She moved here to allow me to be close to my parents and play for the Kingsmen. It's not fair for her to always sacrifice for me if I'm not willing to do the same.

"Don't say no. I think you're right. A live-in nanny is the best option. It'll be weird… I've never had anyone help me with Theo before, but I can't rely on my parents to always pick up the slack. And Bianca and Evan are headed back east for grad school in the fall. A nanny is our best solution."

Having my twenty-two-year-old twin half-sibs help me out with Theo would have been ideal, but they have their own lives.

"Are you sure? God, I've felt so guilty about this."

I squeeze her shoulders. "Han, don't feel guilty. You've

given up a lot of opportunities over the years because of my career. It's just a few months."

Tears pool in the corners of her eyes. "Do you think Theo will be okay with someone else watching him?"

"He's gonna miss you, for sure. But he misses you when you're ten minutes away. We'll video chat with you and school will be starting soon, so he'll be busy all day anyway."

"I guess." She looks down at her hands.

I cover her hands with mine. "Does he resent me when I'm away working?" I arch an eyebrow.

"No... I guess not. But you're a football player. It's different. He's proud of you. He can usually watch you on the television at night and see you at work."

"And you're a nurse who helps people in the worst moments of their lives. I'll make sure he knows who the real hero is out of his mom and dad."

A small smile creases her lips. "Okay, I'll talk to him about it tonight."

I nod. "He's going to be fine. I promise." I squeeze her hands.

"I hope so."

I retract my hand. "So for this nanny thing... what do I have to do?"

"Well... I had heard they can be hard to come by these days. So just in case you were okay with it, I already got in touch with a local agency that handles clients like yourself." There's that look again, the same one from when she asked me to talk.

My forehead wrinkles. "Hot, single, professional athletes with an abundance of charm and charisma?"

"No." She gives me a stern look. "I was talking about celebrity clients. When they interview the candidates, they don't tell them the client's name until they're hired. Then they have to sign an ironclad NDA. Keeps the celebrity hunters away."

I nod. "Makes sense. So you want me to do this?" I try to hide the slight whine in my voice. I hate hiring people. I pawned off finding a gardener and house cleaner for this place on my mom.

Hannah tilts her head and presses her lips together. "I can do it if you want, but it's not going to be me who has to live with them."

"You just said they won't know who they're working for, so it's not like I'd meet them anyway."

"No, but you could view the tapes, tell the agency your preference."

Just the thought of spending hours watching videos of boring British women telling me their beliefs in disciplining a child makes me want to vomit. They'll go by my rules in the end.

"I trust you to make the best decision for Theo."

We share a smile, and she says, "All right. I'll take care of it. But don't come bitching to me if Mrs. Doubtfire shows up on your doorstep."

I chuckle. "You have my word. But could we go a little easier on the eyes?"

She lets her head flop back on the couch. "Do not sleep with the nanny, Brady." One eye opens and glares at me.

"Relax. Everything will be fine. You'll see. You'll come back and everything will be just like it was."

She exhales a huge breath. "I sure hope so."

I'll live with a nanny as long as she understands it's Theo she's watching, not me.

three

. . .

Violet

"Cheers." Amara clinks her wineglass to mine. "Spill it. Which high-profile client's brat are you babysitting?"

I chuckle and take a sip of wine just to torture her a little longer. "You know I can't tell you much."

Amara and I met as freshmen at Stanford and continued on to law school with each other. Only she graduated and now works as a lawyer in a family law firm that represents high-end clients in the city. So she understands the confidentiality clauses in my job.

She waves me off, leans back, and sips her wine. "I'll take what you'll give me. We could play a game of twenty questions and see if I guess right?" Her brilliant blue eyes light up with mischief.

I shake my head.

She dragged me out to celebrate that I got hired as a nanny for a very high profile and important family. I don't even know who I'm working for yet and won't until my NDA is signed right before my first day. But accepting the job puts me that much closer to having enough money for a decent down payment on a small condo—allowing me to escape the confines of my parents' house in Santa Clara.

No twenty-eight-year-old wants to live with her parents, especially parents who have no problem pointing out all the ways you've failed them as a daughter after they up and left everything to move from South Korea to the United States to give you and your brother a better life. Their daily guilt trip.

"Did you get a signing bonus for this one?" She tucks a piece of her chin-length dark hair behind her ear.

"You're the only person who would ask me that." I chuckle.

Amara shrugs. "Gotta ask for what you want. Worst that happens, you'll tell me no."

"Well…"

Her eyes widen.

"I did, but it's going right into my down payment account." I point at her in warning. Last time, she would not accept the word no when trying to convince me we both needed a long vacation with white sand and blue water that came with daiquiris and a lot of half-naked men.

"How are Hae Won and Him Chan doing these days?" She hovers her wineglass in front of her bright-red-lipsticked lips.

Amara always refers to my parents by their Korean names rather than the American ones they took when they moved to the US, Lilly and Grant.

"Oh, you know, lamenting their daughter's life choices while bestowing praise upon their son. One who can do no wrong."

I love my brother, but the way he's regarded in our family just because he popped out with a dick is ridiculous. The fact that he of course became a doctor further makes my life a living hell. I don't even think he likes being a doctor, but my parents do and brag about him to all their friends.

"They'll never forgive you for dropping out of law school." She takes a grape from the charcuterie board we ordered and pops it in her mouth.

"Not in this lifetime. My mom told me it was the biggest disappointment of her life." I raise my wineglass. "Here's to sucking as a daughter." I down a big gulp.

Amara frowns. "Don't let her get to you. You're doing something you love that brings you joy."

"According to my parents, they know best." I spin my wineglass, watching the fluid swish. "Enough about me. How's work going for you?"

"Just the usual this week—cheating spouses, rich guys trying to hide money so they don't have to pay as much spousal support, and heartbroken kids. If anyone was worrying, the American dream is in full effect in the Bay Area."

"Sounds grand."

She shrugs. "I'm not complaining. The pay is good." She winks and downs the rest of her wine.

Amara puts on a front, but there's no way all the sadness and destroyed families she witnesses day in and day out wouldn't get to someone.

———

A few days later, I park my fifteen-year-old white Honda Civic along the curb, finding the address on the stone wall above the front door. Just to make sure I'm in the right place, I pick up the piece of paper from the passenger seat with the address on it.

Yep. This is it.

I shouldn't be surprised. I knew the family I'd be working for had money, what with all the secrecy throughout the interview process and the NDA they kept incessantly bringing up.

I've worked for rich people before—single working mothers rarely hire full-time nannies—but based on the looks of this house, this family is next level. Maybe one of them is some tech company owner. God knows there are enough of them around here.

I love my job. The hardest part is always saying goodbye to the kids once my assignment is over. At first, I enjoyed the short-term contracts—it kept things interesting and they usually pay a little more—but I've been contemplating telling the agency I want a more permanent position.

By the time I turned twenty-eight, I'd expected to have a husband and be starting my own family. But since my disaster of a relationship with my ex, Peter, I've sworn off men. Well, mostly. There is one guy I hooked up with as a rebound who hasn't left my mind, but basically, I enjoy being single. So why not dedicate myself to helping raise someone else's child and watch them grow up?

I push aside all thoughts of the future and exit my car.

The house isn't new money. It's got the architectural charm of a house built over a hundred years ago. All the bushes up the walkway are neatly trimmed and tidy, along with flowers tucked into the dirt. It's beautiful.

My stomach dances. I'm always a little nervous before I meet a family, and especially the child, since that's who is really in charge. Let's face it, if the kid doesn't like you, you're out of a job.

All I've been told about this child is that he's about to be six years old. Apparently the mom must travel for work for an extended period and with the father's schedule, they need full-time live-in help until the mom returns.

The first thing I spot on the way to the door is all the cameras on the roof staring down at me. I knock on the dark wooden door and hold my breath. I hear the pitter-patter of little feet on the other side of the door and someone fiddling with the lock. Another set of footsteps sound. A few seconds later, the door swings open to reveal an attractive blonde slightly older than myself.

"Hi, I'm Violet from the Nanny Pros."

She smiles and opens the door wider to reveal a sandy-haired boy with hazel eyes staring at me. "Hi, Violet. I'm

Hannah, Theo's mom." She presses her hand on the little boy's head.

I bend down so I'm at Theo's level. "Hi, Theo, I'm excited to meet you. I'm Violet."

He takes one step forward, away from his mother. "Do you like Lego sets?" From the expression on his face, my answer is a make-or-break moment in our new relationship.

"I *love* Legos."

"They're the best! I'm working on a NASA rocket. Wanna see?" He holds his hand out and I glance at Hannah.

"Theo's dad will be home any minute. He got caught in traffic."

I nod and accept Theo's hand. "I can't wait to see."

He leads me past several big rooms. Though the house is older, you wouldn't guess from the openness. The decor and furnishings are more modern than traditional. In the corner of the massive family room is a table strewn with bags of Lego bricks and a half-constructed space shuttle at one end.

"Wow. Theo, this is awesome. Did you do this yourself?" I bend to inspect the inside of the shuttle.

"My dad helps." His pride-filled face suggests this is something he enjoys doing with his father.

"You guys are doing great. Maybe I can help you with your Lego sets sometime?"

His smile dims. Shit, wrong thing to say. "Okay, but not this one. This one is just for me and my dad."

"I'm sure we can get another one for just you and me to work on."

He smiles. "Okay!"

A door opens from the back of the house and then voices, but I can't make out what they're saying. I assume it must be Theo's dad and Hannah.

"Dad's home." Theo looks at me.

It's obvious from his huge smile that he worships his dad like a hero. It warms my heart before it chills because I have no idea what that feels like. I've never had that kind of relationship with either of my parents and never will.

I hear the low timbre of a male voice the closer they get to the family room. There's something familiar about it that I can't pinpoint. But when Hannah walks in the room, smiling with her arm outstretched to the man beside her, my stomach plummets and sweat beads along my hairline.

My one-night stand from six months ago stands there. The same man I haven't been able to get out of my head.

At my insistence that night, we didn't exchange names or numbers. I'd never had a one-night stand before and I wanted my one time of wild abandon to be completely anonymous. It made it easier to act out of character and was part of the thrill, if I'm being honest.

But here he stands in front of me.

My new boss.

Theo's dad and… oh my god! Hannah's husband? I slept with the father of my new client.

Bile burns my throat while he and I stare at each other from across the room.

Hannah is introducing us, but I don't hear anything she says because I'm running through our conversation from when I showed up. Was there anything else in the information packet?

Her lips stop moving and she looks at me expectantly.

I open my mouth and my cheeks heat, embarrassed that I have to tell her I wasn't listening. But the man by her side catches on and steps forward with his arm outstretched.

"Violet, right? Brady Banks."

I take his hand hesitantly, mostly because of his satisfied grin, like an FBI agent who just caught the guy he's been chasing for a decade. When our palms meet, the heat sears my skin and an electric current runs up my arm.

Suddenly, there's a flash in my brain of the night we spent together and those hands running all over my body, cupping my breasts and trailing down to—did that finger have a ring on it? A tan line?

Think, Violet! Think.

"Daddy, Violet is gonna help me with a Lego set. But don't worry, not the rocket ship. I told her that one is ours."

I blink back to the present as Brady ruffles Theo's hair. "Thanks. For a moment I thought I was replaced," he teases and looks at Hannah with a shared smile.

They have their "I know what you're thinking" faces on and a cool sweat coats my body. How do I get myself out of this?

"You seem a little shell-shocked, Violet." Hannah giggles. "Don't worry, Brady gets that reaction a lot, don't you?"

He glances at her a little sheepishly... guiltily? "Comes with the territory of being the Kingsmen's best wide receiver."

I didn't know who he was when I met him. At least not in the context of being a professional football player. I don't follow sports. My dad wasn't the type of man to sit around on a Sunday and watch football. He spent his Sunday going to church and doing everything that needed to be done around the house before his six-day workweek began on Monday.

"The hiring process was really hush-hush. It's a bit of a shock when I find out who I'm working for when they're in the public light. Sorry." I hope my smile masks my sudden discomfort.

He nods. "Understandable. We didn't want women taking the job just to get close to me. Some women are hard to beat off." He raises his eyebrows at me. A direct dig since I didn't want to exchange any personal information that morning.

"Jeez, Brady," Hannah mumbles and rolls her eyes.

It doesn't faze Brady as his gaze travels down my body with so much heat my nipples pebble under my shirt.

Hannah clears her throat. Brady glances at her and then Theo.

"Sorry I was late. There was a pileup on the 101 and I got caught in traffic." The sexual tension disappears as if a magician snapped his fingers.

"It's no problem," I say.

Brady looks between us all and shoves his hands in his pockets. "How about I give you the tour and show you where you'll be sleeping? Han, can you hang with Theo for a bit?"

At first, I panic. Is he trying to get me alone so he can make sure I don't tell his wife about what happened between us? Then I realize this is likely the first of many times I'll be alone with this man. "Sure, that'd be great."

He gestures for me to go first. "Do you have bags with you?"

"They're in my car."

He leads us up the wide stairway to the second level. "I'll help you with them after."

We pass a few bedrooms and head up another set of stairs to a third level, where he leads us out onto a balcony that has a majestic view of the city and the bay and the Golden Gate Bridge in the distance.

"Figured we'd start at the top and work our way down." His wolfish grin smiles down at me.

We stand there for a beat, staring at the view. I don't know about him, but I'm filled with angst and awkwardness. Are we going to address the obvious?

Finally, he speaks. "You didn't really have any idea who I was, did you?"

"No. I don't follow professional sports." I shake my head. "Is Hannah your wife?"

His jaw tightens. "Are you asking if I was married when we slept together last year?"

I glance behind me, paranoid that someone will overhear. "Let's not dodge the question. Are you married?"

He shakes his head and narrows his eyes. "I've never been married. Hannah and I aren't in a relationship. We haven't been for many years. She's here only to meet you." He pushes a hand through his hair. "You seriously thought I was cheating when we hooked up?"

It's obvious he's irritated by my assumption, but when you find out your fiancé was a serial cheater, it doesn't seem like a stretch that the guy you met one night and went home with might be.

"She's the one who let me in your house. She's the mother of your son. It's not completely ridiculous for me to think that. Also, you did insist we go to a hotel and not back to your place."

He steps forward and his expensive cologne accosts me in the best way, woodsy and something undeniably male. "That's because I don't bring women back to the house I raise my son in."

My hands fly up at my sides. "I don't know you at all." We both stare at the door and I lower my voice. "I didn't even know your name until five minutes ago."

"Whose fault is that?" He holds my stare for a beat then walks past me. "This is the balcony. I don't let Theo up here by himself."

He heads back into the house, ignoring we're anything other than boss and new nanny. I stand there for a beat before following, lamenting the fact that I've only just arrived and have already pissed off my new boss.

four

. . .

Brady

I show Violet—at least I know her damn name now—
around the rest of the house, including her bedroom. It
sits exactly opposite my bedroom on the far side of the staircase. Had I known my new nanny was the woman I've been
obsessing over the past six months, I would have given her
the bedroom farthest from mine.

It's as if someone took my brain, shoved it in a blender,
then stuffed it back inside my head. My thoughts race like
cars on a highway, flying back and forth in a thousand
different directions. To make matters worse, I'm still insanely
attracted to her. When I shook her hand after Hannah introduced us, I physically reacted to her touch—as though a lightning bolt raced up my arm. I know she felt it too. I could tell
when her pupils widened.

But then she doused that with a bucket of cold water
when she asked whether I was married. What the fuck? As if
I'd ever do that.

I feel her eyes on me as we make our way through the
house, and I point out everything she needs to know. It's a big
house, so it takes quite a while, but relief fills me when we
rejoin Hannah and Theo in the family room.

"How'd the tour go?" Hannah is cuddled up with Theo on the couch watching *Hey, Arnold*. I'd swear she knows by her smile, and that brings up the question of whether or not I'll tell her. I don't keep anything from Hannah and this directly relates to Theo. Or does it?

I glance furtively at Violet.

"Good." She nods and smiles. "It's a big house, but I'll get the lay of the land soon enough. And Theo will help me, won't you?"

His gaze darts from the TV to her. "Yep! My dad says I'm a great helper. Did you see all my Lego sets in my room?"

"Just really quick. Did you want to show them to me?" Violet asks.

He bounds up off the couch. "Yeah, come on. I'll show you my favorites."

Violet glances at me as if for permission, and I nod.

We watch them leave the room, then Hannah turns to me. "Well? Spill."

Shit. I knew she knew. I swallow hard. "Spill what?"

She stands from the couch. "What do you think of Violet? Think you can live with her for a few months?"

I exhale because Hannah has no idea what a loaded question that is, but relief swamps me. At least she didn't pick up on anything weird between me and the new nanny. "She seems nice. Theo obviously likes her and that's what's most important."

"Yeah, while you were showing her around, he was telling me all the things he wants to show her and do with her." Tears fill her eyes and she sniffles.

"Hey, what is it?" I sit next to her.

She blinks a few times to clear her tears. "Maybe I should decline the job offer. A few months is a long time to be away from him."

"Hey…" I take her upper arms in my hands. "It's not that long. This is a great opportunity for you, Han. Theo will be fine. You'll still talk to him practically every day, and one day, he'll be proud to know that his mom was off helping people who really needed it. You're doing a good thing."

"But what if he resents me because I'm gone so long?"

I squeeze her arms. "He won't. I'll make sure he knows what a superstar his mom is." I dip my head down and smile at her.

A small smile tilts up the corners of her lips. "Thanks, Brady. Though it'll never be like having a professional football player for a dad."

I chuckle. "Well, I do have the coolest career ever." She laughs, but I let the humor fade. "I know it's useless saying this, but try not to beat yourself up. Theo will be fine. He knows his mom loves him."

Her face crumples and a fresh set of tears floods her eyes. "I'm going to miss him so much."

I pull her into a hug and run my hand up and down her back. "It'll be fine. *He'll* be fine, I promise."

She sniffles and squeezes me harder.

"Mommy, why are you sad?"

Theo's voice from behind me causes me to pull away from Hannah. I turn to see him and Violet, her eyes wide as she soaks in the scene.

"I'm okay, sweetie," Hannah says, wiping her eyes.

Theo frowns. "But you're crying." He climbs into her lap.

"Mommy is just going to miss you." Her hands cradle his face and she stares at him for a beat too long. He grows antsy.

"Why don't you give her a big hug?" I urge him.

Theo wraps his little arms around her and squeezes tightly, his head buried into her neck.

I glance at Violet, who's looking between Hannah and me. "You guys good here for a bit? I need to run over to my mom and dad's."

Hannah looks up from Theo. "Yeah. I was hoping to stick around as long as I could if that's okay?"

"Hey, I know it's my day, but why don't you take Theo to your place for the night?"

Her smile grows wider. "Really? Are you sure?" She stands with him clinging to her like a koala bear.

"Of course. I'm sure he'd love to spend some extra time with you before you go, right, buddy?"

"Yeah!" Theo squeezes her tighter and Hannah laughs.

"All right then. I'll stick around here until you get back though, in case Violet has any questions," Hannah says.

I force myself not to turn and look at the woman in question. "That works. I'll see you guys in a bit then."

I leave the room as if a murderer is chasing me down, snag my car keys off the table in the foyer, and drive away from the house as fast as is safe, needing to put some distance between me and the only woman I've never been able to forget after our night together.

———

My parents only live a couple of minutes from me, so when I let myself inside, my head is still spinning. In fact, I think maybe I'm about to reach blaring red light panic mode.

I hear some noise from the back of the house, so I follow the noise, hoping to find my dad. It's not that I don't want to speak to my mom, but her advice will probably be to bang it out. I mean that literally. That's probably the exact phrasing she'd use too. And though I love the thought of sleeping with Violet again, I'm looking more for my dad's practical wisdom at the moment.

When I enter the room, my brother, Evan, is spread out on the couch, playing video games. He looks at me, nodding toward the television. "Hey, man, you want in?"

I shake my head. "I'm looking for Dad. Know where he is?"

"Think I heard Mom say he's in his office."

I leave the room without saying another word.

"Who pissed in your protein shake this morning?" Evan calls after me.

I walk upstairs and down the hall to my dad's office. I open the door, too preoccupied with everything in my head to knock. "Dad, I have a problem."

Three sets of eyes turn to me. Shit. Lee Burrows, the quarterback for the Kingsmen, and his girlfriend, Shayna, are sitting across from my dad.

"Oh shit, sorry. I didn't know you were in a meeting. Hey, guys." I raise my hand in hello and they return the gesture.

I know why they're here. After the deal for my parents to buy the Kingsmen went through, I talked to my dad about the situation with Lee's girlfriend. She used to be on the Kingsmen staff as an athletic trainer but was let go last year after her relationship with Lee came out in the press. I told my dad how good she was at her job and that she's the one who nursed Lee back to health after his injury last season, and he said he was going to offer her old job back to her. I assume that's why they're here.

I turn my attention to Lee. "Looks like I managed the grand gesture, Burrows. Getting your girl her job back and all." I wink.

Lee shakes his head, and I'm pretty sure if my dad wasn't here, he'd tackle me to the floor right now.

"Go ahead, Lee, kick his ass," my dad says.

"I'll be in the kitchen." I go to shut the door.

My dad stands. "Everything okay, Brady?"

I look between him, Shayna, and Lee and blow out a breath. "You guys might as well hear it too." I step in and shut the door. After transferring last year, Lee's been one of my best buddies on the team, and Shayna and I formed a quick friendship when she'd taped me up last season. "The new nanny Hannah hired? It's the woman from that one-night stand who wouldn't give me her number."

"The gymnast?" Lee asks, eyes wide.

I laugh and bite my inner cheek. "Can you fucking believe it?"

"No," he says.

"Me either. It's like a romance novel." I shake my head.

"What am I missing?" Shayna asks.

Lee looks at me with a serious expression. "You can't kiss the nanny, Brady Banks."

I point at him. "And that's the problem."

"Will someone please explain what the hell is going on?" My dad's voice is stern. He doesn't like being one of the few people in the room who doesn't know what's going on. It's his control issues.

I push a hand through my hair and flop down next to Shayna on the couch. "Last year... probably six months ago, I had a one-night stand with a woman who wouldn't give me her name or any detail about herself. That same woman just showed up to be Theo's live-in nanny."

My dad's lips press together. "That's unfortunate."

"Or fortunate," Lee says, positioning himself to face me. Shayna does the same. "Brady's been going on about this girl for months, wondering how he might be able to track her down and see her again."

I glance at my dad and see he has a single eyebrow raised. "And she's a gymnast as well as a nanny?"

I glare at Lee. He snickers. I tell my dad, "No, that's just an... inside joke."

I'd referred to Violet as a gymnast in humor because she was so damn flexible that night.

My dad nods knowingly but is kind enough not to press the issue. "Are you still attracted to her?"

My hands fist in my lap. I bite my lip and nod.

"Why don't you just hire another nanny?" Shayna asks. "Then you can pursue the gymnast." She cringes when she says the word gymnast, probably assuming I'm one of those guys who tells all about my conquests.

I shake my head. "Hannah's leaving in days. I can't tell her we need to find a new nanny because I slept with the one she hired." Jesus, the coincidence. You'd think I've nailed every woman in the Bay Area for something like this to happen.

"Why not?" Shayna asks.

My shoulders sag. "Because she'd deny the opportunity for her career and I can't do that to her after she's moved twice for my career. This is supposed to be her time and I cannot be the one to take that away from her. I'm just gonna have to deal with blue balls for a few months."

"Sounds like something to look forward to." Lee smirks.

I flip him off.

"Have you and the... gym—nanny discussed what happened and how you'll need to set aside any possibility of repeating the nature of your relationship until after the job is complete?" my dad asks in his most professional manner.

"No, I gave her a tour and bolted out of there. Hannah's there with Theo." I glance at my dad's clock on the wall.

"Well, that's a conversation you need to have, Brady. If there's one thing I've learned after being married to your mother all these years, it's that it's best to confront these things head-on. They can be uncomfortable for everyone involved, but in the end, it's less complicated and better that way."

I chuckle. "That's because Mom has no filter."

He grins. "You're not wrong there."

I sigh and sink deeper into the cushions. "I know you're right." I groan. "I'll do it tonight after Theo and Hannah leave for her place."

He nods and smiles. "I'm sure it will be fine."

Fine. That's not exactly the word I would use to describe it.

Agony is more like it. Living for months lusting after the woman in the bedroom across from mine. Living in the same house, sharing space like we're a pseudo couple.

Yep. Everything will be agonizingly fine.

five

. . .

Violet

I'm in what is supposed to be my bedroom with the door open, sitting on the comfortable chair in the corner, reading the new thriller I bought yesterday. I hear a noise on the main floor. Brady must be home.

Hannah and Theo left for her house fifteen minutes ago. I wasn't sure what to do with myself. I don't want to unpack my bags because there is a good chance once Brady returns, he's gonna give me the boot. Wandering around the house by myself didn't seem fitting, nor could I figure out how to turn on the TV with the fancy sound system anyway, so here I am.

My hand tightens on the book when his footsteps land on the stairs. I still when his footsteps stop on the landing. I hold my breath when his footsteps make their way down the hall.

He appears in my doorway and all the air rushes from my lungs. Good Lord is this man hot. Dressed in cargo shorts and a T-shirt that clings to every one of his muscles, he looks every bit the hot AF playboy he knows he is.

"Hey. We should talk."

I nod, my voice lodged somewhere I can't find.

He steps into the room and glances at the bed, clearing his throat. "Maybe we should chat downstairs."

"Okay... sure." I set the book on the table beside the chair and stand.

He motions for me to exit first, so I do, walking ahead of him and feeling his gaze on my back. My mouth is dry by the time we reach the family room and I sit on the couch.

Brady sits in the chair to my left. And then silence. He rests his forearms on his thighs, his hands clasped together. "Obviously, I had no idea who you were before you came. Hannah took care of hiring you, so I was just as surprised to see you as you were to see me when I walked in."

I'd figured as much from his startled look of confusion. "I know. And for the record, I had no idea who hired me. They keep the names secret until I sign an NDA for their high-profile jobs."

He chuckles and leans back, relaxing in the chair. "Yeah, that much was obvious."

My cheeks heat. "Do you think Hannah noticed?"

He shakes his head. "No, she doesn't know we've slept together and..." I'm not sure what he's going to say. "I'd like to keep it that way." Brady studies me as though he thinks I'll disagree.

I hold up my hands. "Fine by me." It's not like I can afford to go back to my employer and say I slept with the father so can I have another family? Just imagine the horror. We're silent for a beat and I decide to use the opportunity to do what I should have done the moment he left the house earlier. "I want to apologize for the question about whether you were married or not. I shouldn't have assumed, it's just..." I don't want to get into my relationship history with him.

"Just what?" His head tilts, and I shake mine.

"Nothing. I just want to apologize."

"I overreacted. If I were you, I probably would have thought the same. You don't really know me, so I can't blame you. Especially when Hannah was the one to meet you at my house. Our situation is... not typical of other co-parents."

Definitely not. They have a shared affection, but it's not romantic love. I want to be nosy and dig into that statement, but I don't want to feed this feeling of what I'm positive is jealousy in the pit of my stomach. I have no claim over Brady. I wouldn't even give him my name or number after we slept together.

"Anyway, seems like we're going to be roomies for the foreseeable future, so I thought we should clear the air. Get all the awkwardness out of the way. Hannah being gone is going to be hard on Theo, and I don't want any uncomfortableness with me and you to add to that."

I blow out a relieved breath. Guess that means I'm not fired, which I tell myself is a good thing. I need the money this job will provide.

"Well… we're adults. I'm sure we can manage to put… what we did aside." My cheeks heat under Brady's gaze. Suddenly, I wonder if he's also having visions of himself pounding into me while he holds me against the wall.

He clears his throat and shifts in his seat. Maybe he is. "Exactly, we're adults. And we did an adult thing together, but that doesn't have to make it weird."

God, this situation is awkward. Especially when he's clearly avoiding saying the word *sex*.

"Right, not weird at all." I give him as natural a smile as I can muster.

"We're in agreement then? We won't mention this to Hannah—or Theo obviously—and we'll carry on as if what happened six months ago never occurred."

I understand why he doesn't want Hannah to know, but something about his request irks me just the same. Knowing it's probably just my past trauma popping out of its bunker and waving hello, I push away the feeling. I didn't have an affair with Brady. He wasn't married when I slept with him. We never fell into a relationship afterward either.

"You have nothing to worry about, Brady. Wait... do you want me to call you Mr. Banks or Brady?"

He looks a little uncomfortable for a beat, then answers, "Brady."

I nod and stand from the couch, wanting to end this awkward conversation. "I guess I'll go get my things from my car and unpack then."

Brady stands too, forehead creased. "You didn't do that already?"

With a shrug, I say, "I thought you might fire me as soon as you came back."

He chuckles and rocks back on his heels.

"With the way you ran out of here..."

Brady nods and pushes a hand through his hair. "No, I get it." Then he walks toward the front door. "I'll help you bring them in."

I quickly follow him. "Oh, that's okay. I can handle it."

He stops and spins around, spearing me with a look that reminds me of the intense gaze he had when he was over me, fucking me.

Jeez, am I some sex addict now or something? My brain has only one track since I arrived in this house, and it has everything to do with Brady Banks naked.

Brady doesn't say a word and continues through the large home toward the front door.

Great. He's going to see my beater of a car. I mean, I knew he'd see it eventually, but I was hoping I wouldn't have to bear witness to his expression.

Because I've been putting most of the money I make into my savings toward a down payment to move into my own place, I've neglected my car. I should probably buy something newer and more reliable, but every time my mom starts in on me about Peter, I'm reminded why I need to own a place.

"I parked on the road because I wasn't sure if I should park in the driveway or not."

He stops and I almost stumble into his back. "Oh, well, why don't you pull into the driveway? Just park on the right-hand side and I'll use the left. That way we can each come and go as we please."

I nod. "I need to grab my keys from upstairs."

He crosses his arms. "I'll wait."

"Great." With a sigh, I head back to the staircase. I suppress a shiver, feeling his gaze on me.

Better get used to it, girl. This is your life for the foreseeable future.

My first night at the house is okay, though it's weird to be there and not have a little one to take care of.

Brady and I pretty much avoided each other for the rest of the night. I hung out in my room and unpacked and read. At one point he came up to say that he was making himself some dinner and asked if I wanted some, but I declined. Not because I wasn't hungry but because I wasn't sure I could trust myself around him yet without having wayward thoughts.

So I ate the protein bar in my purse, but when I awoke at five thirty this morning, my stomach hurt from lack of food. And caffeine.

I slip out of bed and slide my feet into my knit slippers with pom-poms on them to go make some toast and coffee. Brady's bedroom door is still closed when I walk quietly down the stairs and into the kitchen.

I allow myself a moment to enjoy the view of San Francisco out of the large windows. I can't imagine what this house costs to have a view like this.

My stomach growls and I remember why I came down here. While no one is around, I peruse the cabinets and drawers, figuring out where Brady keeps everything. Being a nanny, the kitchen is usually where I spend most of the time.

I find the bread and the toaster relatively easy and slide in two pieces of bread and press down. I grab a plate and search the counter for his butter dish. After scouring the entire surface of his grand kitchen, I open the fridge and there it is, cold and hard.

What kind of sadist puts their butter in the fridge? All it will do is tear up my toast.

Brady has one of the überfancy cappuccino makers, so I decide to give it a go. I've worked for a lot of rich people, so I'm not new to these high-end machines, but I've never used this particular brand before.

I do what I think I'm supposed to, but that doesn't work. No matter which button I press, the machine doesn't start. After a few minutes, frustration wins, and I let out a growl.

"She can be temperamental."

I whip around at the sound of Brady's voice, covering my heart with my hand. Holy crap, he's all sweaty. His bare chest glistens under the stream of sunlight pouring in through the window.

"You scared me."

"Sorry." He lifts a water bottle and squirts a stream of water into his mouth. The shirt he must've been wearing while running dangles from the back of his waistband.

"I thought you were still sleeping."

He shakes his head and walks over to the large island, where he sets down the water bottle. "Bet you didn't guess I'm an early riser."

"Oh." That makes two of us. I sure hope Theo is too. Otherwise we might have some awkward moments.

"Want a hand?"

I'm not sure what expression I'm sporting, but it takes him nodding at the cappuccino maker behind me for me to remember what I was doing.

"Yes, please. I've used these machines before, but I can't figure yours out."

He walks around the expansive island. "Yeah, you have to handle her with care."

"Her?" I raise my eyebrows.

He slides in next to me in front of the machine. "When she gave me problems, Theo was three and suggested I name her." Brady chuckles, reliving the memory. "He thought maybe it didn't like not having a name and since then, it stuck."

I smile. "So, what's her name?"

"Glinda."

"Glinda... so proper."

Brady shrugs. "I let Theo choose. He was really into *The Wizard of Oz* back then."

"Well, if you can introduce Glinda and me, I'd be most appreciative."

"Sure..."

While Brady goes about showing me how to turn Glinda on and how to adjust all the settings and exactly what they mean, I listen intently, but it's hard when the hottest man I've ever known stands beside me. Especially a man I've been in bed with and I know how it feels to have him on top of me.

He reaches across me and his shoulder brushes mine. I'm acutely reminded that I'm not wearing a bra because my nipples pebble at our skin-to-skin contact as though my cells remember this is the man who gave us the best orgasms of our life.

Brady stills for a second and I wait for some smart comment to come out of his mouth.

God, this is so awkward. Hopefully it will get better as time passes and we grow more accustomed to being around each other day in and day out.

"I think I've got it, thanks." I give him a wan smile, and he steps back to give me room to make one myself. I follow by memory everything he told me to do and the machine whirs to life and hisses. "Success!" I smile wide and raise my hands over my head, looking at him over my shoulder while the machine does its thing.

He gives me a funny look I can't decipher. "Great." He drags his palm along the back of his neck, and I purposely keep my expression neutral when his pec twitches and his lower abdomen flexes. "I'm gonna go shower."

I nod, unable to say anything because my mouth is as dry as a cotton ball.

Once he's out of the room, I slump against the counter. This is going to be a long few months. Good thing I packed my vibrator.

six

. . .

Brady

The big day finally arrives—Hannah is leaving.

We all stand by the open front door, delaying saying goodbye as long as possible. I've got to hand it to my kid, he's trying to put on a brave face when I know he's breaking. During my season, Theo spends the most time with Hannah since I'm traveling so much. But he's become quick friends with Violet, so hopefully she'll cure some of the heartbreak.

What's not to like? Violet has a killer smile, hot body, is cute as fuck when she's embarrassed—which seems to happen easily and often—and smells incredible.

Okay, those better not be the same qualities my son likes in her, but they're definitely the ones that draw my attention.

"And be sure to take pictures of his first day at school, okay?" Hannah says to me, tears in her eyes.

"I already told you I would. Like, five times."

"I'll make sure to text you some pictures every day," Violet says, smiling at Hannah from a safe distance, trying to give us some family privacy.

"Oh, that would be wonderful. I might not be able to reply every day and depending on the time change when I get them, I might not text you right back, but know that I appreciate it." She turns to say something to me but then returns her attention to Violet. "And make sure he gets a good breakfast before school. No sugary cereal or anything like that, otherwise he'll be crashing by the second hour."

"I'm sure Violet knows what she's doing, Han. This isn't her first nanny job." I squeeze Hannah's shoulder. I know this is all her nerves and second thoughts talking. "We'll be fine."

"Promise?" Her bottom lip twitches and she's close to bursting into tears.

"Promise." I draw her into a hug, and she squeezes me so tightly I grunt. When I pull away, I catch Violet's eye for a moment, and she's looking at us kind of strange. "Now... go make the world a better place. I'm proud of you."

She hugs me again before turning her attention to Theo.

"Mommy, do you have to go?" Theo asks, the first tear dripping down his face. He held a good fight there, especially for a five-year-old.

My chest squeezes. I hate seeing Theo upset and I know Hannah does too.

"Mommy won't be gone that long, buddy. You'll see the time will fly by."

Theo flicks his gaze my way as if to question what Hannah said. I run my hand through his hair and nod.

"I'm going to miss you so much." Hannah falls to her knees in front of him. "But we will talk all the time on video chat, okay? Just like when Daddy is on the road."

He nods, but the tears stream down at a rate his hands can't stop them. "I'm going to miss you, Mommy."

That sentence makes Hannah's tears burst forward, leaving tracks in her makeup. "I'm going to miss you so much." She pulls him into her, giving him a tight hug.

Theo's little fingers grip the back of her shirt as if he's afraid she's going to vanish in a flash.

My gaze meets Violet's and holds before we both look away, giving them some privacy.

Hannah draws back. "I have to go catch my plane." Her voice is shaky. "You be good for your dad and Violet, okay? I'll call you as soon as I land."

Theo nods, pressing his lips together as though he doesn't trust himself to speak.

Then Hannah gives him a kiss on the cheek, wiping his tears away with her thumbs, and stands. "Good luck," she says to Violet. "Thank you."

"I swear I'll treat him like my own," Violet says.

Hannah nods and squeezes Violet's hand. "I believe you." Then she swipes under her eyes and sniffles. "All right, time to get myself together. I'll see you all in a few months."

Theo comes to me, wrapping his arms around my legs, while Hannah makes her way down the driveway to the car driving her to the airport. I pick up Theo and hold him close.

He buries his head in my neck and mumbles, "I don't want Mommy to leave."

I run my hand up and down his back. "I know, buddy."

"Your mom is doing such a great thing. She's helping all kinds of people who have no one else to help them," Violet says, walking toward us.

"Does that mean my mommy is brave?" Theo asks her.

"Very brave."

The three of us watch as the car reverses down the driveway, and we wave until the taillights are no longer in sight.

Theo bursts into tears, so I continue rubbing his back and telling him it will be okay. My chest squeezes in knots from seeing him so upset, but I remind myself it's temporary. Once we get into our new routine, he'll adjust fine. Especially once he realizes he still gets to "see" Hannah on our video calls.

"What do you say we go open that really cool Spider-Man Lego set we've been saving for a special occasion?"

Theo perks up in my arms, lifting his head from my shoulder. "Really?"

"Yes. I don't have to be anywhere for the rest of the day,

and I think Glamma and Grandpa are going to stop by, so if we start now, we can probably finish it before they get here. Then you can show them."

His smile is already full of pride as though he's finished the set. "Let's go, Daddy." He wiggles out of my hold, and I set him down before he races back to the family room.

Violet chuckles. "I see you're familiar with the art of distraction."

We both move away from the door. "Parenting 101. When you don't know what to say to make it better, bribery is best."

"Seems like maybe you'll teach me a few things while I'm here."

My mind quickly goes to a dirty place. God, there's so much I could teach this woman, but none of it has to do with parenting techniques.

————

Theo and I are cuddled on the couch and watching *Hey, Arnold* when the doorbell rings. We finished the Lego set an hour ago and have been chilling since. Theo is still pretty glum because of Hannah leaving.

"I'll get it," Violet calls from the kitchen. She said she was going to make dinner. I'm not sure if she feels uncomfortable with me being home. It's odd for me to have someone in the house when I'm here with Theo.

I don't think much of her answering the door. Probably a package—until I remember my mom and dad said they were going to stop over to cheer up Theo.

I fly up from the couch. "I'll be right back, okay?"

Theo nods absently, not diverting his attention from the TV. I could've told him I'm going to cut my heart out with a butter knife and his reaction would've been the same.

I've been dreading this moment. The moment Violet meets my parents.

Not because I'm embarrassed by my parents and not because I don't think they'll love Violet, but because I'm unsure whether my dad told my mom I slept with Violet.

I asked my dad not to mention it to my mom, but if I've learned anything over the years, it's that they tell each other everything. There are no secrets between them, and I've always admired that until right this moment. And if my mom knows there's something between Violet and me, she's likely to bluntly comment on it or say something that makes Violet uncomfortable. I love her, but that's how my mom is. She can be a lot if you don't already know her.

Violet already has the door open, and my parents are inside before I make it to the foyer.

I try to act as nonchalant as I can, giving them hugs and kisses. "Hey, Mom and Dad." Afterward, I step aside and wave my arm toward Violet. "I see you've met Violet."

"We were about to before you interrupted," my mom says. "Hi, Violet, I'm Brady's mom, but you can call me Lennon."

"Nice to meet you." Violet smiles.

My mom sizes her up then looks at me with a sparkle in her eye. I let out a sigh of relief because she doesn't know; otherwise she would have made a comment like "the sample being so good you couldn't get enough" or "one taste and you just slid right in."

"And I'm his dad, Jasper." My dad holds out his hand, and she shakes it. "Nice to meet you, Violet."

My mom rolls her eyes. "Always so formal. This isn't a business deal, Jasper. This is the woman who'll be caring for your grandson for the next few months." She leans forward. "How did it go?" She cringes because we all know this won't be an easy transition for Theo.

I shrug. "How you expected. He's pretty bummed." I nod toward the family room. "Television is our savior at the moment."

My parents nod. My mom looks at Violet. "You look spry

and young and flexible. You'll be able to keep up with his energy. Be thankful for that." She touches her hip. "I swear I need a hip replacement already. The other day I caught myself before falling down the stairs and I haven't recovered."

My dad smiles at her.

"What? I told you about it."

"Yes, and you act like you're eighty-five." He kisses her lips. Great, PDA in front of the new nanny.

"I'll take that as your promise to massage it tonight."

"Only if—"

"*Dad*!"

They both laugh, and Mom's eye sparkles with amusement as she says to Violet, "It's so easy to get Brady all riled up. Now, where is my grandson?" She claps her hands together.

"In the family room. Ask him about his Lego creation." I shove my hands in my pockets.

"Great. Come on, Violet, I'd like to get to know you better." Rather than looking at Violet, Mom looks at me with wide eyes, trying to tell me something, but I have no idea what. She'll make her intentions clear soon enough. She always does.

My mom loops her arm through Violet's and drags her toward the family room, asking her where she's from and about her heritage.

My head falls forward in defeat.

"Oh relax." My dad's big hand squeezes my shoulder.

"Thanks for not telling her."

My dad chuckles. "That's what you got from your mom's performance? That I *didn't* tell her?"

"You know Mom. If she knew, she'd probably quiz Violet to find out if I was using every technique she taught me."

My dad cringes and shakes his head, but we both know I'm right.

Growing up, my mom made sure I understood that when I slept with a woman, my first job was to make her come, then I could worry about my own release. She calls it sexual chivalry.

My dad stares in the direction they went. "So... that's her."

I rock back on my heels. "That's her."

"I know I've been busy getting everything in place to transfer ownership of the team over to your mother and me, so I haven't had a chance to follow up, but have you two discussed how to move forward?" He arches an eyebrow.

I nod. "Yeah. We decided to keep it to ourselves and act like it never happened. Be adults about it."

My dad clamps me on the shoulder. "Adults? Okay then." He chuckles for the tenth time since he arrived. "That might be easier said than done."

I bite the inside of my lip. "Tell me about it."

seven

• • •

Violet

B rady's parents are way more down to earth than I thought they'd be from the Google search I did after asking Brady if he was married when he slept with me. Basically, the internet provided me with four main pieces of information about Brady—first was that he's a professional football player for the Kingsmen. Duh. Second, he's a single dad. Third, he's been photographed with A LOT of different women. And fourth, his parents are rich. Like megarich. We're talking one-percenter rich, which I'll admit, as a woman with immigrant parents who worked hard for every penny earned, I found intimidating.

I wasn't prepared for who walked through the door. His dad is an older version of him. A cordial man and not at all stuck up. His mom... did seem different in the photographs. But not bad, just different. Tattoos up and down her arms, short, dark, edgy hairstyle. A pair of cutoff shorts and a tank top that didn't seem to fit the huge diamond ring on her left hand. She even let a few curse words go in front of Theo, which neither Brady nor Jasper blinked an eye about. The best thing was I could tell they were a close family and I got the impression that I'll see them quite a bit during my time here.

I load the final plate from dinner into the dishwasher and turn it on. I wet the washcloth so I can give the counters a fresh wipe down. I'll probably go have a shower and either read in bed or watch TV in my room. The job is always more awkward when the parents are home with you, but when you've had sex with the person, it tends to be a little more awkward.

As I'm squeezing the washcloth out, Brady walks in.

"Theo's out like a light. Only had to read one story tonight." He raises his finger as though it's a win, which it is. He sits across from where I am at the sink on the other side of the island.

I chuckle because that's a thing with Theo—he always wants another story. If Brady is home, he puts Theo to bed, but in the week since I got here, I had to do it once when Brady was out late. That night, I read three stories before Theo would go to sleep.

"He must've been tired from all the emotion today," I say.

He nods.

Hannah texted about an hour ago to say that she'd arrived safely and would call once she was settled, getting Theo upset all over again.

"I'm sure it will get easier as the days go on, but I feel bad for the little guy," I say, wiping the counter.

His being sad only makes me even more determined to show him that although I'm not his mom, the two of us can have fun together until she returns.

Brady waits until I rinse the washcloth a final time and hang it over the side of the sink before he speaks again. "I wanted to fill you in on something that's going down next week so you're in the loop."

I frown because he sounds serious. Hell, he looks serious. His golden eyes are intense.

"Okay…"

"My parents have bought the Kingsmen Football Team, and they'll be announced as the new owners soon."

I double blink. "Wow."

He looks a little sheepish. "I know that sounds like such a rich kid thing to just drop in your lap like it's nothing."

I chuckle. "Well, yeah. I mean, I can't imagine saying my parents just bought the Los Angeles Rams so…" He smiles. "I just wasn't expecting you to say that. I thought you were going to fill me in on appointments I had to take Theo to or something."

Brady laughs, and god, the way it lights up his eyes reminds me of rain glistening on a gold-colored fallen leaf.

"No, not a dentist appointment." He shakes his head.

I tilt my head and study him. "What's that going to be like for you?"

He shrugs. "They both said they'll do their best to remain impartial where I'm concerned. They've never interfered with my career and only ever give their opinion when asked. My mom much prefers to interfere with my personal life." He rolls his eyes.

"She certainly is entertaining."

"That's one word for it," he says wryly. "Did she offer you a free vibrator yet?"

My eyes widen and I suck in a breath. "Wh-what?" Then I remember what Google said about her having wealth before they got married, but I'm not going to blurt out I know anything about his parents because I spent a whole sleepless night digging up information.

He laughs at my expression. "She must've been trying really hard to be on her best behavior."

"How so?"

"My mom owns a sex toy company, among other things. But the sex toy company is her passion." He waves me off. "She's very… sexually liberated."

"Really? Wow. That's…"

"Yeah, you don't have to finish that sentence or that thought. It is what it is. I took a lot of shit about it growing up, but my mom is an amazing woman, so I tried not to let it bother me too much." He shrugs.

"Women around the world have her to thank for their orgasms." And now I'm thinking about all the orgasms Brady gave me during the night we shared and my cheeks heat.

He chuckles lightly. "Yeah, I suppose they do."

"I assume Theo has no idea?"

Brady shakes his head. "No, he's too young. At some point he will, but not anytime soon. It might be one of the few boundaries my mom respects. They kept it from me for a long time growing up."

I nod. "I can't imagine either of my parents being so open about sex. I never even had the birds and the bees talk with them. My mom just left a book about puberty on my pillow one day. She probably assumes I'm a virgin still and my husband will teach me."

Brady's mouth drops open. "Really?"

I nod.

"I was on the other end of the spectrum. My mom lectured me in high school about how to make sure the girl comes first —all her tips and techniques. It was traumatizing."

I cover my mouth with my hand to keep my laugh in, picturing teenage Brady sitting on the edge of his bed as Lennon used a pointer stick and a whiteboard to go over female anatomy.

"Laugh it up, but we both know it paid off." He laughs too, but a few seconds later our laughter dies, and we're left with our gazes locked. The stifling heat in the room ratchets up. "Sorry, it was just a joke…"

I wave off his concern. "We can joke about it." I give what I hope comes off as an easygoing smile, even though inside I'm strung tighter than a piano wire.

"Right." He gives me a sharp nod.

"Anyway, I think it's cool that your mom made herself a success. I'm sure that couldn't have been easy, especially since it had to do with putting women first."

"Oh, she has lots of stories about how the patriarchy tried to fuck her over, but don't ask her about them or you're in for a three-hour chat."

I smile. "Noted."

"That's sort of how my parents met actually. My mom was trying to get my dad to invest in the company she wanted to start."

"Aw, that's romantic. And then they fell in love and along came you."

Something changes in his expression. He shifts in his seat. "Actually, Lennon's my stepmom, but she's the only mom I've ever known, so I've always thought of her as my mom." He shrugs. "I don't think genetics is the only factor in what makes someone a mother."

"I'm sorry, I didn't realize. Are you close with your biological mom?"

He shakes his head, jaw tense. "You'd think after three decades it would sting less, but it doesn't." He sighs. "My biological mom took off right after I was born. My dad raised me on his own until Lennon came along when I was six."

The urge to reach across the island and wrap him up in a hug is strong, but I have to remind myself that I work for this man. He's my boss.

"I didn't mean to pry." My voice is soft, and I hope he can hear the sincerity in it.

"It's fine. It's not a big secret or anything."

I don't mention Google hasn't picked up on it yet. "Well, I'm glad you had an amazing woman in your life. And I agree, genetics isn't the deciding factor on whether you feel loved and accepted in your family."

He frowns. "You say that as if you know from experience."

"Oh… no. Just saying in general."

I don't know why I don't tell him that he's right—I've never felt as though I fit in in my family. Never felt as though I measured up. Maybe I just don't want to say the words out loud. They'll feel more real that way.

He nods, not saying anything and I'm not sure he believes me, but he seems to be gentleman enough to drop the subject.

"I think I'm going to go have a shower and go to bed." I move to walk around the counter.

He stands abruptly. "Right. Okay. Anyway, circling back… the reason I brought up the Kingsmen thing is because there's going to be a press conference and my parents want the whole family there, so Theo will be coming, but I'll need you to come to keep an eye on him since I'll most likely get pulled away for some stuff with the press after the announcement."

"Of course, no problem."

We sort of stand there awkwardly for a moment as though we're not sure if we should leave the room together or not. After a few seconds, we both walk toward the kitchen exit.

He must be heading upstairs too because he continues alongside me toward the stairs. It's awkward as hell and neither of us speaks because we both know how weird this is. We make our way up the stairs, and when we reach the landing, we head down the hall in the same direction toward our bedrooms.

Eventually we come upon mine and we both stop, turn and face each other. Brady's in front of his door and I'm in front of mine.

"Good night." My voice is barely above a whisper.

"Good night." His voice holds a rough quality I've only heard from him when we were in bed together.

Our gazes hold for a few beats, but I manage to strip mine away and turn around, feeling his attention on me the entire time. I open my door and slide inside, then shut it behind me. I lean my back against the door and my head falls back. I stare at the ceiling.

There's a lot more to Brady than a hot body, sexual prowess, and charm. And realizing this only makes him harder to resist.

eight

. . .

Brady

"Am I gonna have to talk, Daddy?"

I glance at Theo in the rearview mirror. "No, buddy. You just have to stand there, and after the announcement is made, you'll hang with Violet until we're ready to come home."

I glance at Violet sitting in the passenger seat of my Porsche SUV. She looks fantastic and I'm not just saying that because I'm attracted to her. I'd have to be blind not to notice. Her black hair is down and styled in waves. Although she dresses casually at home, she has on an outfit that's more fun and flirtier today—just like the night I met her at the club. She's wearing a hot-pink suit with an oversized blazer that's made from velvet, and her lipstick matches the suit.

"Okay. 'Cause I don't wanna talk to all those people," Theo says, interrupting my thoughts.

"And you won't have to." I get into the right lane to exit the highway toward the Kingsmen's arena.

"Are you nervous?" Violet asks me.

She's been quieter around me since our conversation in the kitchen a few days ago, so I welcome her starting a conversation with me now.

"Not really. I don't much like doing press, but after this many years in the league, I'm used to it." I shrug and move into the left lane to make a turn at the next intersection.

"I can't imagine inviting a whole bunch of strangers into my life and them offering their opinions on what I should and shouldn't do. I can barely handle my parents' involvement." She laughs, but there's a hard edge to it.

I wonder what her family deal is. This isn't the first time she's alluded to some disconnect between her and her parents.

We arrive at the stadium a few minutes later, and Theo is bouncing in his seat. He loves being here because my team-mates give him tons of attention. I show my badge at the gate and park.

"Someone is excited." Violet smiles at Theo as he takes her hand and hops out of the SUV on her side.

I exit, lock the vehicle, and go around back to meet them on the passenger side. "Ready?"

"Yeah!" Theo throws his fists in the air and rushes toward the door we always use.

"Hold up, buddy. We're in a parking lot. You need to watch for cars," I say.

Violet rushes after him and takes his hand while I trail behind. She bends down and whispers something and he nods, securing his hand in hers. There's something natural about her care for Theo. I guess that's why she's a nanny. I don't know if she's like this with all her jobs, but it's obvious to me that she cares for Theo's well-being. She's not just here for the large paycheck.

They wait for me outside the staff entrance, and Theo is explaining something to her as I approach.

"And then the security guard will let us in. Ralph's cool. He even gives me candy."

"Sounds like you've made a lot of friends around here," Violet says.

Theo nods excitedly. "I love coming here. Dad, can we throw the ball on the field?"

I walk up behind him and ruffle his hair. "There won't be any of that today. This won't be like the other days." Reaching forward, I hit the buzzer beside the door.

Theo frowns and looks down at his suit. "No monkey business."

I chuckle. "That's right, but you only have to hang out for a bit. Then you and Violet can go find something to do until I'm done, okay?" He nods. "And Aunt Bianca and Uncle Evan will be here too."

"Yay!" He jumps up and down as the door swings open.

Ralph grins at my son. "Hey, little man. How're you?" He holds up his hand.

Theo jumps to slap it. "Ralph, my aunt and uncle are here today, but Dad said no football."

Ralph glances at me with a grin and reaches into his pocket. "Well, it can't always be playtime. But you know what? I think I have something in here for you." He pulls out one of the Werther's Original candies he always has in his pocket and holds it out to Theo.

"Thank you!" Theo snatches it from his hand and unwraps it. "Oh." He looks at Violet and points with his thumb. "This is Violet." He sucks his candy again.

"She's Theo's nanny," I add.

Ralph nods and smiles at her. "Good to meet you, ma'am."

"You're gonna need to cut off the ma'am stuff, Ralph, or we can't be friends. Violet only, please."

He chuckles, resting his hands on his protruding belly. "Fair enough." Ralph gestures with his head behind him. "Rest of your family is already here."

"Great, thanks."

We walk all the way through the door. I lead us through

the hallways of the stadium until we reach the room my dad told me to meet him in. We open the door and everyone turns in our direction.

"Hey, guys." My mom walks over and gives Theo and me a hug.

"Aunt Bianca! Uncle Evan!" Theo runs over, and Evan grabs him and flips him upside down.

"Good to see you again, Violet," Mom says.

"Same, Mrs. Banks."

"What did I tell you about the Mrs. Banks stuff?" Mom's eyebrows shoot up.

Violet chuckles. "Sorry, Lennon."

My mom winks at her. "That's right. You haven't met my other two kids yet. Let me introduce you." She gestures for my brother and sister to come over while my dad gives us a wave from the corner of the room since he's on a phone call. Evan has Theo hanging upside down by his feet. "This is my son, Evan. Evan, put Theo down." My mom shakes her head.

Evan pretends to drop Theo but catches him, flips him, and puts him down on his feet. Theo can't stop laughing.

"And my daughter, Bianca."

"Nice to meet you," Bianca says. Her long dark hair is pulled back into a slick bun and she's wearing a conservative navy dress.

"Hey, Violet." Evan reaches forward to shake Violet's hand, and his gaze gives away his interest in her.

I clear my throat when he doesn't immediately let her hand go.

"Uncle Evan, Aunt Bianca, swing me!"

Evan laughs. "Sure, but let's move over there where we'll have some more room."

At the same time, Bianca frowns. "Not a good idea, buddy."

He rolls his eyes. "Surprise, killjoy says no."

Bianca crosses her arms. "Have you considered we're going to be on national television and if we're throwing him around like a football, he's going to be all wrinkled?"

"It's okay." Theo pulls at his collar. Getting him to wear dress pants and a button-down shirt this morning took a twenty-minute debate.

"C'mon." Evan nods to his right. "Let's do it over here by the couch."

"It's like you don't hear me," Bianca mutters as she follows him.

"Let's go, Violet." Theo reaches for her hand and drags her away.

My mom stands beside me, silent until the four of them are far enough away that they can't hear us. "She's cute, honey."

"Don't start."

"I'm just saying." She looks at me with wide eyes, trying to sell her innocent look, but I know her. Thank God she doesn't know I've slept with Violet or else she'd be relentless.

I shove my hands in my suit pockets. "Well don't. She works for me."

She shrugs. "You wouldn't be the first man to fuck the nanny."

I press my fingers to the bridge of my nose. "Seriously, Mom?"

"Well, think about it. If it turned into something more than just banging, you already know how she'd be with Theo."

"It could also be a disaster if things went sour before Hannah returns." I raise my eyebrows at her.

She moseys over to a table of treats, grabs a carrot, and takes a bite of it. "Ah, so you've already considered it."

"We're not having this conversation." I walk away without another word, my mom laughing as I head over to say hello to Giles Hanover, the previous owner.

Truth is, the guy is a pompous ass, so I'm happy he won't be the owner anymore.

My mom doesn't follow, probably sensing that I'm done with this conversation. Which is a good thing, otherwise I'm sure she'd suspect that I'm struggling to remember that Violet is my employee, not my plaything.

nine

· · ·

Brady

The press conference goes fine, though we get a lot of questions about me receiving preferential treatment now that my parents are at the helm. We assured the press there won't be, and if they knew my parents, they'd know that to be true. This is an investment for them, and like all the investments they've made, they're looking for a return. My parents are adept at separating business from their personal lives, and I have no doubt that if they thought it was time for me to move on from football, they'd tell me.

Training camp starts in less than a month, so I've invited some of the guys over to work out in my gym. They all live in San Francisco like me, and although we're welcome to use the Kingsmen training facility, it takes close to an hour to drive there.

"Can I get a water?" Chase drops the eighty-pound weights he's using and asks over "Rapper's Delight" by Sugarhill Gang, which plays out of the surround-sound speakers.

I nod toward the small kitchen in the corner of the mirrored room. "In the fridge there. Help yourself."

"Pass me something, man?" Miles says from the treadmill where he's getting started on a run.

"Me too," Lee says from the bench press.

"What am I, a fucking waitress now?" Chase grumbles, tossing them each an energy drink.

"There's a good tip in it for you." Lee winks at him, and Chase rolls his eyes.

"When do we get to meet the gymnast? Oh shit, sorry, I mean the new nanny." Miles laughs and downs half of his bottle.

I wish I'd never told them that about her being like a gymnast. I know Miles enough to know that he's more making fun of me for calling her that than anything to do with her.

I grimace at the weight I'm lifting as I finish my last set of bicep reps, then set down the weights and give him my attention. "Shut the fuck up."

Chase raises both hands. "I can't speak for Cavanaugh, but I don't do sloppy seconds." He winks as if that should make me feel better.

Thank goodness I pushed Violet to take Theo to the park so she can't overhear all this shit from my supposed friends.

"Don't be a pig." I don't like the idea of anyone talking about Violet like that.

"Methinks the man doth protest too much," Miles says, breathless from his run.

"I don't think that's how it goes," I say, walking over and upping the speed on him.

He almost loses his traction but quickly presses the speed back down and flips me off. The problem with having professional athletes as friends is their reflexes are too damn good.

He gives me a "no shit" look. "I know that."

I roll my eyes at my bookworm friend.

"So nothing has happened between you guys?" Lee asks, toweling off his face.

I shake my head. "I told you all, she works for me now. Nothing is gonna happen."

"Yeah, but you also went on and on about what a great lay she was," Miles says. "And you actually searched her out. Does she know she's living with her stalker?" His tone is dead serious, and I throw my empty water bottle at him. Of course he dodges it.

My stomach turns at the thought of these guys knowing intimate details about Violet because *I'm* the one who supplied them with the information. I always thought I was a gentleman because I make sure the women know the deal before we sleep together, but maybe I'm not as much of a stand-up guy as I thought. "Doesn't matter. Theo comes first, and he really likes her. She's great with him. I can't screw that up for him while Hannah is away."

Lee walks past me, claps me on the shoulder, and picks up the sixty-pound dumbbells to do laterals. "You're a good dad."

"Thanks." I don't feel like a good dad when I'm mentally undressing Violet when she bends over to grab a Lego piece or when I'm in my shower, tugging on my cock with memories of our night together.

"He's gonna fuck her," Chase says matter-of-factly.

"I'm not." I pick up the weights again.

"The want you had for her doesn't just disappear, and you haven't even asked us to go out. It's off-season, man, and not once have I received a phone call to head to the clubs." He wipes his face and looks at the others.

"I got Shayna." Lee holds up his hands.

Miles looks at me with a pained expression when he shakes his head.

"This is my time with Theo," I argue.

"That never stopped you on the weekends before," Chase argues. I'm not sure why he wants to fight this out right now.

"Hannah was here," I say.

"You have live-in help!" Chase holds out his arms. "Admit it, you don't want any other pussy. You're happy to sit tight here and watch rom-coms all night."

"Hey now, some of them are good," Lee comments. We all glare at him, and he shrugs, going back for another set. "Come on, you guys, I know you watch them."

Chase shakes his head. I don't think he has ever watched a rom-com, not even with a girl he really liked. If there ever was one.

"You're such a pessimist," Miles says to Chase, stabbing the buttons on the treadmill to slow it to a jog.

"Just a realist. You'll see." Chase grins at me as though he knows he's telling the truth. And I have no fucking rebuttal.

"You ever find out why she wouldn't give you her number?" Miles asks.

I frown and wipe the sweat off my forehead with my forearm. "No. The conversation was awkward enough."

"How's wedding planning going for Twyla?" Lee, always a good guy, changes the line of conversation.

Miles's little sister got engaged almost a year ago, and although he puts up a good front when she comes into town to visit, he's made it clear to us he doesn't like her fiancé.

"Are you trying to ruin my day?" Miles grumbles.

"You're not the first guy to hate his sister's fiancé, but what is it with him?" I ask.

He stops the machine and steps off the treadmill, reaching for the towel dangling off the side. "I tried telling her he wasn't good enough when they first started dating, and it made for a lot of tension between us. She won't listen to me. If I tell her I don't like her future husband, it'll only push her closer to him and further from me."

"They've been together a while, right? Maybe he's matured," Lee says.

"I'm telling you, this guy isn't who he pretends to be. I can feel it. Underneath his happy exterior, there's something more there. I just can't figure out what. But I will before she says I do."

"I get the feeling no one will ever be good enough for your sister in your eyes," I say, making my way over to the fridge to grab another drink.

"Damn straight. It'd be way easier if she were a lesbian. Then I wouldn't have to worry about her being with men who let their dicks make decisions for them. Men are pigs. Myself included."

"What's up, Chase?" I ask. "You don't have anything to add to this? You had lots to say about my situation."

He glares in my direction. "What do you want me to say? It's not my fucking business."

"Well, do you think Twyla should marry this guy?" I grab my drink from the fridge and twist off the cap.

"She can do whatever the fuck she wants. It's a free country."

Miles groans. "Can we stop talking about this? You guys are stressing me out."

I shrug, and Lee says, "Yeah, sure."

"And when she's here next month, none of you better mention this conversation." Miles looks around the room and points at each of us.

I hold up my hands. "My lips are sealed."

"FYI, men who are pigs do change when it comes to their one," Lee says. We all stare at him, and he holds up his hands again. "At some point, you will all be on my side."

"Where? On your island of rom-coms?" I laugh.

"You do know I'm with all the women on the island, right?"

"Fuck that. I like girls who love horror movies anyway." Chase does lunges back and forth across the room.

"Twyla loves them," Miles says.

"I know," he says, grunting when he turns to come back our way.

I cross my arms and stand in his path. "You do? How do you know that Miles's sister loves horror movies?"

Miles's eyebrows furrow as we wait for the answer.

"We talked about one once," Chase says.

"And when did this occur and did you have clothes on at the time?"

"Fuck you, Banks," Miles yells.

I hold up my hands. "I'm just giving shit back to him."

"Well, she loves rom-coms too, so she's not the woman for you." Miles eyes Chase.

Chase laughs. "Yeah, Cavanaugh, I have a thing for your engaged little sister." He shakes his head and turns away from us, doing his lunges.

I glance at Lee because Chase is saying all the right things, but it seems off. Miles grabs a set of weights and holds them at his sides, lunging with Chase while asking about some protein he's been using, apparently oblivious to what Lee and I see.

We move on to talk about our prospects for this coming year and who we think might make it on the team through training camp. When we're done working out, I tell the guys I'll order from the health-nut place around the corner and have it delivered. They have great protein bowls and smoothies on their menu.

After I've placed the order on their app, we head upstairs to the main floor to hang out in the family room until the food arrives. We aren't there for more than a few minutes when Violet and Theo arrive home. Theo rushes from the front door to the back of the house, probably having seen everyone's cars in the driveway. He barrels into the room at full speed.

"Hey, guys!" He jumps on the couch and wedges himself between Lee and Chase.

Theo loves hanging around the guys from the team. I think he looks at them like pseudo dads or maybe even big brothers. But they're always happy to show him attention and he soaks it right in.

The three guys all say hello and give him high fives or fist bumps. Then Violet walks into the room and everyone quiets. Jesus. Could they be any more obvious?

"Guys, this is Violet Park, Theo's nanny." I gesture in her direction but don't make eye contact because I'm afraid she'll see something in them, like guilt.

"Hi, everyone." She raises her hand.

They thaw from their frozen state and say hello, waving. I take care of introductions, and it's almost comical how clueless she is to who I just introduced her to. She has no idea who these men are and how reputable they are in football.

"How was the park?" I ask, acutely aware that the guys are studying our interaction to razz me later.

"It was good. Theo saw a friend."

"Kale," he says, playing thumb wars with Chase.

"Yeah, they sometimes get together. He seems like a good kid except for his lack of wanting to get dirty."

She laughs. "He wasn't into the sandpit."

The guys look as if they're watching a tennis match, their heads turning left, then right, then left, watching Violet and me talk. Even Chase is barely paying attention to his thumb war with Theo.

The energy in the room grows more awkward the longer the silence stretches, but I can't think of anything to say.

Violet glances at the guys who are watching us.

"I won!" Theo screams and jumps on the couch. "I beat Uncle Chase!"

Everyone looks between Theo and Chase, who shrugs. I'm pretty sure he didn't even do it on purpose. He was distracted.

"Theo, come here for a second." Violet waves him over.

He goes willingly, smiling so wide from his win. When he

reaches her, she bends down and whispers in his ear. He nods excitedly, and she straightens.

"Be right back," Violet says.

The two of them leave. I wait until I can no longer hear their footsteps before I whip around in the guys' direction and give them all a lethal stare.

"What the fuck was that?" I whisper-shout.

"Have you taught him new moves? You know I don't believe in letting kids win." Chase scowls right back at me.

"Not that. Jesus, could you guys make it any more awkward?" I shake my head and plop down into a chair.

Before any of them can respond, Violet and Theo return. Violet's carrying a tray, and Theo walks proudly ahead of her with his chin high in the air.

When they come to a stop near the couch, Theo says, "Do you guys want some? Violet and I made them."

I lean forward to look at what's on the tray. I heard them messing around in the kitchen earlier today, but I forgot to ask what they were up to. Spread out on the tray are small, round beige cookies.

"What are they?" Lee asks.

"*Yakgwa*, Korean honey cookies," Violet says.

"They're really good," Theo says. "Try some!"

"I never refuse a cookie," Chase says, and Theo picks a few up off the tray and carries them over to him.

The corners of Violet's lips turn up in an effort not to laugh. "Theo, do you think you can hold the tray? That way, you can carry it over to everyone and let them pick their own cookies?"

He smiles wide. "I'm strong enough."

My chest warms at the obvious fact that he wants to be seen as strong either by me or by all the guys.

"Especially his thumbs," Miles says, and Chase glares while we all laugh.

Violet gently hands the tray to Theo, and he walks around to each of the guys.

"These are amazing," Lee says around a mouthful.

"Really good," Miles agrees.

I'm the last to grab one and I toss it in my mouth and let the sweet flavor bring my taste buds alive. Once I've swallowed, I look at Violet. "These are great, thank you."

Her lips are pressed into a line, and she nods. "I'm glad you all enjoyed them."

And there's that silence again. Theo has dropped the tray on the coffee table and he's asking Lee for a thumb war.

"If you have something you need to do, I can watch Theo for a while. I'm done with what I need to for the day," I offer.

"Are you sure? If you guys are"—her fingers move in the air and it's cute—"in the middle of something, Theo and I can head up to his room and play a game."

"No, I think it's going to be thumb war challenges for a while." I glance at my son and smile.

She doesn't. "Okay, then I think I might go work out before I get started on dinner."

I nod, feeling all the guys' eyes on us again. I can just hear their dirty jokes in my head. "Feel free to use the workout room downstairs if you want."

"That's okay. There's a yoga place not far from here that runs classes all day. I've been wanting to check it out, but thanks." She gives me a tight smile.

"Hot yoga?" Chase asks, and I scowl.

"No." Her voice is stern. "It was nice to meet you all."

"You too," they all say in unison.

Then she leaves the room without another word.

"I get the feeling someone is on her shit list," Lee says to me under his breath.

"What's a shit list?" Theo asks and moves his whole body horizontally to get his thumb in a better position.

Lee gives me an apologetic look and mouths, "Sorry."

"Nothing for you to worry about, bud," I say.

"Theo, you wanna show me what Lego set you're working on?" Chase nods toward the corner of the large room where Theo works on his Lego sets.

I'm thankful for the distraction. It gives me a second to try to figure out what I'm going to say to Violet later.

ten

. . .

Violet

I'm getting out of the car in Brady's driveway when my mom calls. With the mood I'm in, I should ignore the call, but I know she'll only call back until she hears from me.

"Hi, Umma," I say.

"*Annyeong haseyo*," she greets me in Korean.

We're chatting, just basic small talk, as I walk through the door and set down my yoga mat. I need to go have a quick shower before getting dinner started. Holding the phone to my ear, I walk down the long hallway toward the stairwell near the back of the house.

Theo must hear me because he comes barreling out of the family room and wraps himself around my waist. "You're back!"

My chest warms at his reaction. I know he really misses his mom, and he's probably projecting some of those feelings onto me, but I'll take it.

"Who is that?" my mom asks in Korean.

I respond in English so that Theo understands me. "That's Theo, the little boy I'm nannying for." I ruffle his hair, then cover the phone and say to him in a low voice, "I'm going to take a shower, then I'll come down and see you, okay?"

He nods and runs back to the family room.

"I don't know why you're still doing that job," my mom huffs in English now that I've made the switch.

I blow out a breath. "Don't start, Umma. We've been over this a million times."

"Maybe. But I still don't understand. You should be a lawyer."

I hurry up the stairs, anxious for an excuse to get off this call. "You don't need to understand. It's my life."

"You've made that clear." The disdain and disappointment in her tone is something I never forget.

I inhale deeply through my nose and let it out slowly before I respond. "I should probably get going. I just finished a yoga class and I need to have a shower before I start dinner."

She tuts, probably exasperated that I'm making someone dinner when I could have a law degree. I really don't understand it though. She and my father own a restaurant and were able to provide a decent life for my brother and me.

"Always so quick to get off the phone with me."

"It's just not the best time, Umma. I'll call you tomorrow, okay?" Guilt eats at me over the fact I'd do about anything to get off the phone with my mom. But I always come away from any conversation with her with lower self-esteem.

"When will we see you?"

Guilt bubbles up and over. "I'll see if I can swing by the restaurant sometime this week." I don't say house because they're rarely there. Just like when I was growing up, they're at the restaurant practically twenty-four seven.

"Have you talked to your brother this week?" She really doesn't understand when I say I have to go.

I pull some fresh clothes out of my drawers and set them on the corner of the bed. "No, it's been a whirlwind getting this little guy settled. I'll be sure to catch up with him next week though."

I've often wondered whether she ever asks my brother if he's called me.

"Hmmph."

I sigh. "All right, Umma, I really should go."

"See you when you make it into the restaurant, I suppose."

The attitude in her voice makes me want to throw my phone across the room, but if I have to replace it, it will only come out of my down payment money. I squeeze it hard instead.

"See you then." I hang up and toss my phone onto the mattress.

It was probably perfect that I was planning to have a shower after this. I need it to return me to the relaxed state yoga put me in before her phone call.

———

Unfortunately, a hot shower can only do so much. It isn't a miracle worker. I'm already irritable after meeting Brady's friends for reasons I'm not even sure I should be. I still don't know if that's something I want to bring up with him or not. My mom's passive-aggressive call was just the cherry on top of my already crappy mood.

After my shower, I change into black Lycra bike shorts and an oversized T-shirt and head down to the kitchen to prepare dinner.

When I started, Brady explained to me that he has to eat fairly clean with football season starting soon, and once training camp starts, the nutritionists will have strict guidelines for him and will even do all his meal prep for him, if required. So tonight, we're having chicken tacos. Brady can load his with protein and veggies while Theo and I can load ours with cheese and sour cream.

Brady and Theo are throwing a football around the backyard, and I periodically watch them while I prep dinner. It's clear how much Theo idolizes his father. And it's also obvious to anyone who's seen them interact that Theo is Brady's whole world. When I think of the dominant, sexual man he was the night we spent together, he's worlds away from the laid-back, loving man throwing the football to his son right now.

Dinner doesn't take long to prepare, and I call them both in after I lay it out on the table. They come in smiling and laughing.

"Smells good, Violet." Brady smiles as he makes his way around the island. "Let's wash up, Theo."

Theo walks over to where his dad stands in front of the sink and steps up on the stool. Brady turns on the water, and he helps wash Theo's hands before handing him a paper towel and washing his own. When they're done, they throw away their paper towels as though Theo is Brady's mini-me and walk over to the table. I can't strip my eyes away.

Once Theo slides into his seat, I sit. "Do you need help putting your taco together or are you good?" I ask him.

"I can do it." He grabs a tortilla off the plate in the middle, hoisting himself onto his knees on the chair, and pulls the bowl of ingredients he wants closer to him.

Brady sits beside me and directly across from Theo. I didn't realize that would be the case when I claimed my seat the first night I got here. I'm still not sure which is worse: sitting across from Brady and having a direct view of his gorgeous face the entire meal or sitting beside him where I can feel his body heat.

As soon as Theo puts all the ingredients in the middle of his taco, he folds it in half and brings it up to his mouth—causing everything inside to slide out the bottom onto the plate. Brady and I laugh.

"Why don't you let me fold it for you so that doesn't happen, buddy?" Brady slides his chair back and walks over to Theo. He uses a spoon from one of the bowls to scoop everything on Theo's plate back into the middle of the tortilla, then he folds the bottom and rolls it tight before handing it to Theo.

"Just hold it like that, and you should be okay," I say when Theo looks at me with a look that says he's concerned it'll fall apart again.

Theo takes his first bite as Brady makes his way back beside me. "There you go."

Brady insists I make my taco first, so I do, trying to eat it as daintily as one can when you're trying not to get sour cream on your face or have the whole thing fall into your lap.

He takes his first bite and moans, making the space between my legs thrum with a low-grade tingle. That sound reminds me of the moans he made when we were kissing and I brushed up against his erection.

Once he's done chewing, he asks, "Have you always been such a good cook?"

"It's just tacos." I set down mine and reach for my glass of water.

"Yeah, but everything you've made has been really good."

Theo's chewing but nodding vigorously.

"My parents own a Korean restaurant in Santa Clara, and I spent a lot of time there growing up. You pick up some tips over the years."

Brady opens his mouth to say something, but before he can, Theo pipes up. "You were speaking weird before?"

I smile at him. "I was speaking Korean because I was talking to my mom."

He smiles wide. "Like the cookies."

"That's right. My parents are from South Korea, so when I was growing up, they mostly spoke Korean at home, so that's how I learned."

"Were you born in South Korea?" Brady asks.

I shake my head and pick my taco back up. "No. My older

brother was born there, but they came here when he was three and had me here about a year later."

Dinner continues with Theo asking me all kinds of questions about South Korea and asking me how you say certain words in Korean. His interest in something he doesn't know about is really sweet, and I'm happy to answer what I can.

In the back of my mind, throughout the entire dinner, I'm ruminating over what happened earlier in the day when I met Brady's teammates. I'm still trying to figure out how I feel about it. Because from the way they all stared and watched us interact, they know. And if they do, I don't know what to think about that.

Part of me is angry. It makes things weird. But part of me understands. I told Amara about my night with him, so who am I to be upset? Still, the idea of Brady bragging that he's bagged the nanny doesn't sit right with me. I think I need to bring it up before it becomes a wedge between us.

One thing I know for sure is that I don't ever want to be the person in the dark again. I have to ask Brady, even if it will make things weird and uncomfortable. I just hope he doesn't get upset with me for bringing it up.

As we're wrapping up dinner, Theo washing his hands from all the taco grease, I shift in my seat to face Brady. "Would we be able to chat for a minute after dinner?"

He blinks a few times. I think I caught him off guard. "Yeah, sure. I'll help you clean up. Theo, why don't you go up to your room and play?"

"No cleanup?" he asks.

"Not tonight. You're free." Brady's tone of excitement makes Theo think he's been gifted something rather than not included in something.

"No take backs!" His little footsteps run up the stairs.

I take a couple of plates over to the island to rinse off and put in the dishwasher. Brady follows suit, so I stay at the sink and rinse all the dishes, then put them in the dishwasher. We clean in silence while I work up the nerve to speak what I have to say. Finally, after seeing Brady glance at me nervously more than a few times, I let it out.

"They know, don't they?"

Brady's hand stills on a Tupperware lid, and he sighs. He looks at me, guilt shining so clear in his eyes as if they're made of glass. It's obvious I'm right, based on the fact that he didn't even have to ask me what the hell I'm talking about.

"Why do they know?" My mouth presses into a thin line, and I turn off the faucet and lean my hip on the island. "Did you brag to them after I showed up that you'd already fucked the nanny?"

He cringes and finishes closing the lid on the container. "Are you serious? Funny that you always assume the worst of me. First you thought I was married, and now you think that I ran and told my teammates I've fucked the nanny like some adolescent pimple popper?"

His harsh words cause my fingers to grip the towel in my hand harder. "I'm not assuming anything. I'm asking."

He steps closer to me and stares into my eyes for a moment. "They know because after our night together, I couldn't get you out of my mind and I was pretty much obsessed with the idea of trying to track you down. I even went back to where we met a few times to see if I might run into you. They've been busting my balls for six months because I was so hung up on the mystery woman I had a one-night stand with. So yeah, when you showed up here to be Theo's nanny, it threw me, and I went to talk to my friends about how I was going to handle it. And maybe I shouldn't have told them you were one and the same, but I swear I only told them because I didn't know how to be around you when I still wanted to fuck you."

I stare into his hazel eyes. That was not what I expected to hear. Like, at all.

Brady cringes and rubs his palm along the back of his neck. "Say something."

I open my mouth and close it. Open it again. Close it. Finally, I manage to speak. "You really thought of me that whole time?"

God, why does my stomach flip over when I think about the fact that Brady Banks has been thinking about me, *obsessing* if his words are to be believed, ever since we slept together last year?

He gives me a deadpan look. "Enough that my friends have been relentlessly mocking me for over six months."

I bite my lip to stop my smile from emerging, but it doesn't work. I never thought I would have earned a mention to anyone in Brady's life after we were together. After all, he probably did that kind of thing all the time with women much hotter and more fulfilling. He gave off that vibe and made it clear he wanted to keep things casual before we left for the hotel. Which is what made him perfect for a rebound lay in my eyes.

I wasn't going to be the stupid girl who attached feelings to the two of us being physical together, but it's clear to me now that Brady felt that insane connection between us too.

Which feels amazing.

But isn't.

Because I work for him now. And there's a little boy involved. And I am not ready to risk my heart for another man yet.

"I figured you didn't think of me even once after our night together." I hold his gaze.

He shakes his head. "I wish that were true."

We stand in silence, staring at each other for a few moments.

"Did you think of me after that night?" His question comes out with an air of vulnerability I haven't heard from him before, and it's enough that I can't lie to him, no matter the cost.

"All the time."

The air fills with thick tension. It's one thing to have slept with Brady, but it's another for both of us to admit that there are lingering feelings and we're still attracted to one another.

"Why wouldn't you give me your number that night?" he asks.

The heat building in my body chills with his question and the reminder of why I was in the headspace to sleep with a stranger in the first place.

"I had my reasons."

He arches an eyebrow. "Which were?"

"Honestly, I'd prefer not to talk about it."

A look of complete disappointment flashes across his face. "Did you not enjoy it?"

I laugh because that's the furthest from the truth. "I did."

His eyes widen and he pushes a hand through his hair. "That's hardly a ringing endorsement."

Truth is, it was the best sex of my life, but I don't want to admit that to him. He's my boss, and no matter what, we can't cross that line again. Besides, we shouldn't be discussing this. Reliving those moments won't help keep them in the past. "It was fine."

"Fine? Jesus." He's genuinely despondent. "I know I'd had a little bit to drink that night, but I wasn't drunk. Is that why you didn't give me your number? Because it was that bad for you?"

"Brady—"

"Were you faking it every time you came? I swear if we did it again, I'd make you come twenty times but just with my mouth and hands."

My mouth drops open.

"I didn't mean it to come out vulgar like that. Fuck." He grips his hair. "I just meant that I could make it good for you.

I tried to last time, but maybe I was being selfish from the drinks I had?"

I touch his shoulder. Little electric pulses travel up my arm. "Listen—"

I'm saved from spilling the real reason I didn't give him my number by Theo barreling into the kitchen. "What's taking so long, Daddy?"

Brady looks between Theo and me as though he's torn on who to give his attention to, but I'm happy to take the out.

"You go ahead. I'll finish cleaning up."

He presses his lips together but nods, murmuring, "We're not done with this conversation though."

"I think we should be." I give him a meaningful look.

After a beat, Brady nods, then walks away.

Thank God. Because the only thing worse than having already slept with your boss would be admitting to him that he's the best sex you've ever had and you really, really want to do it again but are trying to be the bigger person.

eleven

. . .

Brady

A few weeks go by, and I try to bring up our conversation about why Violet wouldn't give me her number, but she shuts me down each time. She clearly doesn't want to talk about it, and rather than being some pervy boss trying to force his employee to talk about sex, I let the topic drop.

But it doesn't mean that I haven't gone over that night a thousand times in my head, dissecting her every moan and breath, wondering if she was putting on a show for me but wasn't really feeling it. Could I be that wrong about the connection I thought we had?

Today is the first day of training camp, and though Violet and I have been cordial since our awkward conversation, we haven't exactly been conversing a lot. In fact, we've mostly been avoiding one another unless Theo is around.

Which is why I'm surprised to find her in the kitchen this morning. She knows I get up early too, and Theo isn't up yet.

"Morning," she says breezily. "I made you some protein balls and a fruit plate. Figured it'd be a good way to start the first day of training camp."

Violet looks good this morning. Her hair is pulled back

into a ponytail and she has a white button-down shirt on with shorts.

But I shouldn't be noticing her legs at all.

I clear my throat. "Thanks, that's nice of you, but I normally don't eat before the first day of camp. I'm too amped up."

"Oh. Okay, well, I guess Theo can have it when he wakes up." The corners of her lips tilt down.

"Sorry, I'm just too nervous. It looks really good though."

She shrugs and pulls open the drawer with the cling wrap. "It's not a big deal. Honestly."

Great. As if things weren't awkward enough with us, now I feel like a total asshole.

Violet covers the plate with cling wrap and sets it aside. "Can I get you anything before I make my own breakfast?"

"No, you go ahead and feed yourself."

She nods and walks over to the pantry, opens the door, and disappears inside.

I make my way over to the fridge to grab a water but stop when I hear what sounds like grunting and a yelp from the pantry. With a frown, I peek inside to find Violet on her tiptoes, trying to get the large bag of oatmeal from the top shelf. She's managed to coax it halfway off, and it's about to tip over and fall. I have visions of the heavy bag falling on her head, so I rush in behind her and grab it.

She stills in front of me, and it takes me a moment to realize that her back is pressed to my chest and my groin is millimeters from brushing against her.

"I didn't want it to fall on you," I say by way of explanation.

"Thanks." Her voice is breathy and reminds me so much of our night together that I have to bite back a moan.

Slowly, I lower the bag into her hands. Once she has a hold of it, we stay in that position, neither of us moving, both of us breathing heavily in the small room.

I should step back.

I *need* to step back.

But something keeps me in place.

Whether it's the fact she hasn't bolted or her labored breaths or the sweet smell of her shampoo, I don't know. But my legs feel physically incapable of moving.

Slowly, oh so slowly, she turns around, clutching the bag of oatmeal to her chest, and she looks up at me with those big dark eyes that make me want to do things to her. My tongue slides along my bottom lip and she bites hers. I groan from the tightness growing in my pants. She sucks in a breath, and without thinking of all the many reasons why I shouldn't, I lean in inch by inch, giving her the chance to push me away or smack me across the face to tell me no. But she does none of those things. Instead, she meets me halfway. The moment our lips touch, it's like the firing of the starting gun in a race.

The bag of oatmeal drops to the floor with a heavy thud. My hands are in her hair and her hands are wrapped around my waist. Our tongues meet, and at the taste of her, some part of my subconscious exhales as though it's found what it's been searching for all these months since we were first together.

When she feels my hard length push against her, she moans into my mouth and I can't resist any longer. I need her. Here. *Now.*

I pull my hands from her hair and undo the buttons of her shirt, never letting my mouth leave hers. My cock is practically throbbing, desperate for some attention, but there's not a chance in hell I'm getting off before her. I don't know why she wouldn't give me her number, but if it was because she wasn't satisfied, I'm going to prove to her how wrong of a decision that was.

Once all the buttons of her shirt are undone and the fabric is splayed open, I bring my hands up to cover her breasts, rubbing her nipples through the lacy white bra. Her hand moves into the hair at the back of my head and tightens its hold when I tweak her nipple between my thumb and forefinger. She lets out a breathy moan and I'm about to lower my mouth to her breast when the front doorbell sounds.

"You have to be shitting me." My head falls forward, defeated. "Shit."

Violet stills. "Who's that?"

I don't let her go, but I straighten to my full height. "That'll be Lee. He's giving me a lift, remember?"

Violet's car needed to get some work done, so I offered to let her use my vehicle for the day since she promised Theo she'd take him across the bridge to Muir Woods. Lee doesn't live far from me, so I asked him if he minded swinging by to get me.

"Oh my god." She frantically buttons up her shirt.

"You might have to get it." I gesture at the tent in my pants.

"This is bad. This is really bad," she says as she rushes out of the pantry, smoothing her hair down.

I try to get my head in check, but my hard dick won't listen. I think of dead puppies and Hannah giving birth to Theo—I was not prepared for that view—and that time in college when I played four really shitty games in a row, and finally the hardness subsides.

With a deep breath, I walk toward the front door. It's closed, Lee having gone to wait in the car, I suppose, but Violet is standing near it, wringing her hands and looking at me as though she's waiting for me to fire her on the spot.

"He said he'd wait in the car."

"Listen, about what just—"

She holds up her hand. "We don't need to discuss it. It shouldn't have happened, and it won't happen again."

I bite back the urge to argue with her because she's right. It shouldn't happen again. It would only complicate things— for Theo and me.

So instead of saying what I really want to say, I nod, and without another word, I brush past her and make my way outside, where I flop into the back seat of Lee's vehicle. "Sorry, guys. I was in the middle of something when you came. Didn't see your text."

Shayna gives me a funny look from the passenger seat.

"Something or someone?" Lee puts the vehicle in reverse and backs down the driveway.

"How's it going with the new nanny anyway?" Shayna asks, turning in her seat to face me.

I blow out a breath and flop my head back against the seat. "I am an asshole, and I am thoroughly fucked."

No need to expand on my statement. That about sums it up.

twelve

. . .

Violet

The following morning, I'm up before Theo and in the kitchen again when Brady walks in, dressed in athletic pants and a T-shirt for another day of training camp. As uncomfortable as it is for us to be alone together, I have no choice. My job is to have breakfast ready for Theo when he wakes up.

He arrived home after dinner last night and I managed to make it so that I was never alone with him so we wouldn't have to discuss what happened in the pantry. I didn't want to talk about it, but Lord knows butterflies were in my stomach every time I thought about it during the day.

It was even better than I imagined. The pressure of his lips, the taste when he swept his tongue into my mouth, and the feeling of his hard body and generous arousal pressing against me. I felt like an addict—he was all I thought about yesterday and last night in bed.

I'd almost pulled out my vibrator but refused out of sheer stubbornness. But when he walks in freshly showered, hair still damp, with his T-shirt clinging to his muscles, I realize my mistake. I should have taken the edge off because this is pure torture.

"Good morning!" My voice is way too chipper and I cringe.

If I can't play it off like it wasn't a big deal that we made out yesterday, he will surely want to talk about it. But if I can sell the idea that I'm unaffected, then maybe we can both act as if it never happened.

He stops and studies me for a beat before he goes to the fridge and grabs a water. "Morning."

"You want me to whip anything up before you head out?"

My car is good to go now, so Brady can drive himself to training camp today.

"I'll have some of that fruit if you don't mind." He gestures to the strawberries and melon I'm cutting.

"Help yourself." I hold out the cutting board between us.

He picks up a strawberry and tosses it into his mouth, then grabs a piece of melon.

I place the cutting board on the counter. "Do you want me to pack some to take with you?"

"Nah, this is good."

I go back to cutting up strawberries, and silence falls like a thick blanket over us.

Finally, Brady breaks the silence. "What are your plans for tomorrow? I'm hoping I can ask you a favor."

I set down the knife and turn to face him, leaning a hip on the cupboard. "Brady, you don't have to ask me what I'm doing. That's not how this works. I'm employed by you, so you tell me what you need from me, and I follow your orders."

He squeezes the bridge of his nose. "Do you even hear the words coming out of your mouth? You can't say stuff like that." He sounds as if he's in pain.

"What do you mean?" My forehead wrinkles. "It's the truth."

He raises his head to look at me. "Forget it." He shakes his head. "I'm hoping you can drive into Santa Clara to bring Theo to training camp for an hour or so. He loves being there when we practice, and I cleared it with Coach."

"Oh, sure. Of course I can. Any particular time you want him there?"

He thinks for a moment. "How's eleven? We'll be out on the training field by then."

"Sure. Would you mind if I take Theo to my parents' restaurant afterward for lunch? I've been meaning to swing by there for a few weeks but haven't found the time. It's not that far from the stadium."

"Of course not." He smiles and grabs another strawberry.

"All right then. Just let me know where I need to go, and we'll be there." I pick up the knife and slide some melon and berries to the corner of the cutting board for him to take.

He nods slowly, studying me. I know before he even opens his mouth what he's going to say. "We need to discuss yesterday."

My knife goes down too hard on a strawberry. "There's nothing to talk about."

"Violet." He steps closer to me and sets his hand over the one holding the knife. "You know there is."

I suck in a breath. "Can't we just pretend it never happened?" I turn and meet his eyes.

"Can you?" He arches an eyebrow.

"I can if you can," I lie.

A muscle in his jaw tics and the hand still over mine twitches. Then he gives me a curt nod and steps back. "Okay, if that's what you want."

"It is." I almost manage to convince myself.

Brady's lips press into a thin line. "All right then. You guys have a good day. I'll be home after dinner again, but I'll be able to tuck Theo into bed."

I cut the next strawberry. "Sounds good."

He leaves without another word. Once I hear the echo of the front door closing, I finally release a long breath.

I hate liars. Hate lying to myself. But it's for the best—for the both of us.

———

The next morning, Theo and I arrive at training camp a few minutes before eleven. Most of the security staff know who he is as we make our way through the training facility and out onto the practice field. Theo's holding my hand and skipping along, and I have to hold him back from full on sprinting onto the field when he spots his dad.

"You really like being here, don't you?" I ask, smiling at the way his big eyes are so full of wonder as he watches the men on the field.

He nods a bunch of times. "I'm gonna be a football player like my dad when I grow up."

"Is that right?" I smile.

"Yup, and my dad and I will play on the same team, and we'll win the Super Bowl every year." He nods, not a doubt in his little head.

I don't bother ruining his dream by telling him there's no way he and his dad will ever play on the same team. It's adorable how much he idolizes Brady. And the funny thing is, I don't think it has much to do with what a good football player Brady is, but more to do with how attentive and loving he is.

We watch from the sidelines for a few minutes, and my eyes only focus on Brady. I've never seen him in his football gear, and let me tell you, the tight pants are working for him. I want to take a bite out of that ass. The way he moves around the field so fluidly, weaving in and out of the empty spaces between the shirted players is impressive, even though I know very little about football.

One of the coaches blows a whistle and tells the guys to take a break. Obviously, Theo knows this moment because the little guy runs onto the field toward his dad, who scoops him up as soon as he sees him.

"You must be Violet." I turn to my right to see a pretty blonde with big blueish-green doe eyes standing beside me. She's wearing leggings and a Kingsmen shirt that looks more like an official uniform than fan gear.

Smiling beside her is a woman with olive skin and dark hair and dark eyes. I've never met either of them, and I'm not sure how they know my name.

"I am…"

The blonde sticks out her hand and I take it. "I'm Shayna, Lee Burrow's fiancée." She nods toward the field. "The man in the red mesh shirt. I'm also one of the athletic trainers for the team."

"It still feels so weird to hear you call him your fiancé," the brunette says.

"It just happened a few days ago," Shayna says to me with a wide smile.

"Oh wow. Congratulations." I smile at them both.

"I'm Bryce." The brunette gives me a small wave since she's not close enough to shake my hand. "I work for the *Chronicle* and cover the Kingsmen, so I'm just here for work."

"It's nice to meet you both."

"I saw you with Theo, and I wanted to come over and introduce myself. Lee mentioned that he's met you a few times, and Brady only ever has good things to say about you." Shayna has a sweet demeanor. Her smile appears genuine, but I can't help but wonder if she knows what went down between Brady and me—past and present.

But I decide to take her at face value. "Well, that's good to know. I'm really enjoying working with Theo. He's a great kid."

"He has a lot of energy, that's for sure," Bryce says,

looking out onto the field where Brady's put his football helmet on Theo's head. It's entirely too big and keeps flopping from side to side as he runs around his dad and the group of players talking to each other.

"That's for sure. I'm beat at the end of the day from trying to keep up with him."

The three of us watch in silence, then Shayna turns my way again. "Listen, Bryce and I have plans to go out on Saturday for some drinks. Nothing crazy, but we wanted to see if you wanted to join us?"

"Oh." I'm surprised by the invite and my face must show it because Bryce laughs.

"There's a lot of testosterone around here and over at Brady's, I imagine. Figured you might enjoy a ladies' night out." Bryce shrugs.

"And we didn't know if you're from around here or if you're far from home. I moved here last year and if Bryce hadn't taken me under her wing, I'd probably still have no female friends here." Shayna laughs.

That's actually really sweet of them both. Although I'm not the most social of people, I find myself not wanting to say no in case I come across as rude. I have Saturday night off, but I'd mentioned to Amara that we should do something. We don't have any concrete plans, but I'm sure she wouldn't mind if we had a bigger group.

"I am from around here, but sure, I'd love to come. The only thing is that I made tentative plans with a friend of mine for Saturday night. Mind if she comes along too?"

Shayna beams and looks a little relieved I said yes. "Of course not. The more, the merrier."

"Great."

"Do you have your phone on you? Let's exchange numbers and I'll text you the details."

We pass one another our phones and input our info. As I'm passing mine back to Shayna, Brady and Lee approach.

"Why do I get the feeling you three are up to no good?" Lee says and looks at his fiancée as though he wants to devour her.

"Because you're a smart man," Bryce says.

"Shayna and Bryce invited me out on Saturday night," I say to Brady, gauging his reaction. Will he be upset that I'm infiltrating this part of his life?

Brady's gaze flicks to the two women and I swear a muscle in his jaw tics, but he smiles. "Sounds like fun."

"Oh, it will be." Bryce waggles her eyebrows.

"Where's Theo?" I ask, changing the subject.

Brady nods behind him. "With Miles."

I look over Brady's shoulder and see that Miles has Theo up on his shoulders, doing squats.

"Show-off," Bryce grumbles.

"You don't like Miles?" I've only met him briefly that one time, but he seemed like a nice guy.

"Well, Bryce insists she hates him," Shayna says and rolls her eyes. I get the feeling that maybe she thinks that's not the case.

"Hey, go easy on my man. He's a good guy," Lee says.

Bryce huffs. "I gotta get back to work. I'll see you ladies on Saturday." She walks farther down the sideline and approaches a group of players.

"Me too. It was good to meet you, Violet. See you this weekend."

I give her a smile, and Shayna and Lee head off in the opposite direction that Bryce went, leaving me with Brady.

"Are you sure you don't mind me going out with them this weekend?" I ask.

His forehead wrinkles. "Why would I?"

I shrug. "I don't know… I just wanted to be sure you didn't feel like I was invading your territory or anything."

He seems surprised, but before he can say anything, Theo

shouts from the field, "Violet! Watch how far I can throw the ball."

I smile and wave so he knows I'm watching. Jeez, I'm so distracted by Brady it's as if I forgot I have a job to do. I need to remember that's the only reason I'm here—my job.

thirteen

. . .

Brady

Training camp is more grueling than the regular season, and it takes some time for my body to become accustomed to the grind—even when I take pretty good care of myself in the off-season. Every year that passes, my body feels the difference. At thirty-two, I'm not old, but I'm becoming football old. I can see why most professional football players don't make it to their forties in the league.

I'm so tired that when I head downstairs on Saturday morning, I find that I'm the last one up. Theo and Violet are already in the family room and she's helping him with a puzzle. Since today is my day off, I'd planned to spend it with Theo. I love playing football, but I hate when the schedule doesn't allow me a lot of time to see my son.

"Morning."

"Morning," Violet says and spares me a quick glance.

"Hi, Daddy. Look, I'm almost done with this puzzle."

I step over to the coffee table where they're working and see that it's a puzzle with a picture of a bunch of Lego characters. I don't recognize it, so I assume Violet must have picked it up at some point.

"Good job, buddy." I ruffle his hair and smile at him, then I turn my attention to Violet. "Sorry I'm up late."

"No apology necessary."

"Yeah, but it's your day off." I cringe and push my hand through my hair.

"It's not a big deal. I don't have plans until later, and I wouldn't be up and out of the house by now anyway."

"Okay, well, I'll still make sure it doesn't happen again."

She waves me off, then looks down at the puzzle and does a little clap when she sees that Theo has finished it. "Excellent job! That only took you"—she pulls her phone from her back pocket and looks at it—"ten minutes and thirty-seven seconds."

Theo's head whips in my direction. "Wanna try and beat me, Dad?"

"How about you let me grab some breakfast first? I got a text from your aunt and uncle and they're planning to swing by to hang out with you in a little bit."

Since Evan and Bianca are about to head off to school on the other side of the country, they want to spend time with him before they leave.

"Yay! I can show them the Lego set we finished this week."

"Do you mind if I go grab something to eat?" I ask Violet.

"Go. It's my turn to try to beat Theo's time." She rubs her hands together as if she's a villain, which is almost laughable since she's the kindest, most patient woman I've ever met. She's also the sexiest, but according to her, I'm not supposed to notice that.

I head into the kitchen and fix myself some oatmeal, then at Violet's insistence, I go upstairs and have a shower and change. When I come back down, I can tell the twins have arrived just from the decibel level of the TV.

Evan must've turned on some video game for him and Theo to play because that annoying music that plays on a loop on all those children's games rings out through the house.

I walk into the family room and am surprised to find Violet still there. I figured once my siblings arrived, she would've headed off to do her own thing. But I immediately figure out why she stayed, and it has me clenching my hands at my sides.

"So, what do you do for fun, Violet?" Evan is sidled up beside her on the couch while Bianca and Theo are playing the video game.

Violet shrugs, seemingly unaware that my brother is trying to chat her up. "Yoga, hang out with friends. I enjoy hiking on some of the trails around here."

"Maybe we should try yoga together sometime. I'll bet that kinda thing makes you really flexible, right?" He arches an eyebrow.

I clear my throat to make my presence known. "Leave her alone, Evan." I grab the remote from the coffee table and turn down the volume on the TV.

My brother raises his hands in front of him. "What? I've heard yoga is really good for the body."

Bianca scoffs and shakes her head. "Yeah, right."

"Besides the fact that I'm pretty sure Violet isn't looking to date a college kid, she works for me, which makes it inappropriate. Leave her alone." My voice is stern, and I'm surprised I don't burst into flames from the hypocrisy of that statement.

A quick glance at Violet has her avoiding my gaze, but her cheeks pinken.

"I don't mind an older woman." He leans into Violet's side.

"All right, that's it. Get up." I walk over to stand by Evan's side and motion for him to get off the couch.

"What? Are you serious?" He looks me up and down incredulously.

"Very. Go sit on the chair and leave her alone."

With an annoyed look, he stands and flops himself into the chair to our right. I take the seat he vacated.

"I need to get going anyway." Violet stands. "I have a couple things to do, and I want to see if I can squeeze in a yoga class before getting ready for tonight."

That's right. She's going out with the girls tonight. I almost forgot. "Of course. Thanks for stepping in to help this morning."

"It's no trouble." She barely spares me a glance. "Bianca, Evan, it was nice seeing you again."

They return the sentiment, and after saying bye to Theo, Violet leaves the room.

Theo beats Bianca in the video game, and she grumbles in defeat, then tosses the controller to Evan. "You're up. I hate these stupid games."

He catches it with one hand. "That's just because you can't beat your five-year-old nephew."

"Hey," Theo pipes up.

Bianca smiles and ruffles his hair. "Sorry, bud, but you are five."

Theo wiggles from her hold and goes to sit on the floor near Evan. For whatever reason, he likes to be near the person he's playing.

Bianca slides onto the couch so she's sitting beside me. "How was the first week of training camp?"

"Tiring, but that's to be expected." I relax and stretch one arm across the back of the couch.

"That's because you're getting up there, old man," Evan says with a snicker.

"Shut up."

"Daddy! You said a bad word." Theo doesn't take his eyes off the screen while he reprimands me.

"Sorry, buddy." I glance at Bianca, who's snickering.

"Does he do that every time Mom curses?"

I shake my head. "Just me."

Bianca laughs. "How does it feel to have Mom and Dad as your bosses now?" Her voice is taunting, and I narrow my gaze. She laughs again. "What? I'm just wondering."

"Sure you are." I shake my head a little. "So far, it's been fine. They promised me they wouldn't interfere any more than they would with any other player, so I have high hopes it won't be an issue."

"I could never work for Mom or Dad," Evan says, fist-pumping when his score pulls ahead of Theo's.

"Not sure you could work for anyone."

My brother is a lot like my mom—impulsive, a free spirit, and difficult to control—whereas Bianca is more like my dad —thoughtful, measured, and serious.

"True enough." He doesn't argue.

Evan plays with Theo for a while so Bianca and I catch up, and eventually Theo announces he has to poop.

"Buddy, remember how I told you that you can just say you have to go to the bathroom? You don't have to tell people that you're going to poop."

"Sorry, I forgot," he yells over his shoulder as he rushes from the room, holding his butt.

"Kids are so weird," Bianca says after he's gone.

"So, what's up with you and your hot nanny?" Evan asks with zero segue.

I scowl in his direction. "What's that supposed to mean?"

He gives me an amused laugh. "There's clearly something going on. Or at the very least you like her."

My hand tightens on my knee. "She works for me."

"Yeah, so?" Evan shrugs. "You're very protective of her."

"You were kind of weird when Evan was talking to her," Bianca whispers.

I sigh. "Nothing is going on." I won't be telling these two about the night I shared with Violet.

"You just want something to be going on then? Because

you were acting like a jealous boyfriend when you came in and saw me talking to her." Evan arches an eyebrow.

I scowl. "I was not. And I don't really find you a threat if I did want her."

"You were actually. I'm just trying to figure out if you've already banged her or if it's wishful thinking on your part." Evan never knows when to shut the fuck up.

I grip the bridge of my nose between my thumb and forefinger. "Jesus, Evan."

"She's really pretty," Bianca says as if that would make it okay to lust after my son's nanny. "And nice, and she seems great with Theo."

"She is all of those things, but nothing's happening between us." I look between the two of them.

Evan perks up. "Great, so you won't mind if I ask her out then?"

I practically growl at him. "Evan…"

He chuckles. "No more objections. You want her." He leans back in the chair with a smug look.

Am I that transparent?

fourteen

. . .

Violet

I head downstairs to the kitchen just before nine. I'm nervous about tonight. Shayna and Bryce seem really nice, and Brady assured me that they are, but the first time out with a group of new people is always a little nerve racking. Thank God Amara will be with me.

I couldn't decide on what to wear and I opted for my black, vegan leather strapless dress. It's a little more boring than what I'd usually go out in, but it fits me like a glove and is pretty short, so it's sexy. I'm not sure what Shayna and Bryce would think of my loud style, so I opted not to go with one of my crazier outfits tonight. I did sass it up a little by pairing it with ankle-length black fishnet socks and four-inch black slingbacks though, so there's still a lot of me in the outfit.

Theo is already in bed and the TV is on in the family room when I make my way downstairs, so Brady must still be up. I feel rude just leaving, so I stick my head in to say goodbye.

My heels don't hide the fact I'm approaching, so as soon as I step into the room, his head turns in my direction. I wish I had a camera filming his reaction when he sees me because his eyes widen and he looks me up and down. His lids grow heavy, making every feminine part of me tingle.

"Hey." He stands off the couch. He's wearing a thin pair of dark-gray lounge pants and a white T-shirt that stretches across his many lean muscles.

"Hi. I just wanted to let you know I'm heading out." I gesture with the clutch in my hand to the hallway behind me. "I'll probably be back late, but I'll make sure to be quiet when I come in so I don't wake you guys."

"Yeah, okay. You, ah… you look really good." He swallows hard and runs his hand down the back of his head.

A warm feeling invades my chest. "Thank you."

"You always dress so different when you have an event."

I can't tell from his tone whether he perceives this as a good thing or a bad thing.

"I've always loved fashion and my job doesn't allow me to wear much more than comfortable clothes, so I like to express myself when an opportunity arises." I motion to my outfit.

He nods, rubbing his palm against his five-o'clock shadow. "Makes sense."

We stand sort of awkwardly for a beat. "Well, I better get going. I don't want to leave Amara on her own if she beats me there. I'm going to wait outside for my Uber."

"Right, well… have a good night."

"Thanks, you too. I'll make sure I'm up with Theo in the morning. I know you have to head to training camp early."

"Sounds good. I'll see you at the end of the day then." His eyes continue to run over my body.

Maybe a night in would be better.

I nod and spin on my heel, hyperaware that my ass almost hangs out of my dress and my shoes are clicking on the floor at what feels like an obnoxiously loud level.

Once I'm outside the house, I let out a long stream of air. Putting aside my attraction for Brady is getting harder and harder, especially when he looks at me as if he wants to lick every inch of me.

———

An hour later, Shayna, Bryce, Amara, and I are sitting around a table, sipping drinks and getting to know one another better. We've already gone through the basics of what we each do for a living, where we live, and what our relationship statuses are, and we're moving on to other topics.

"I texted Twyla to join us since she was supposed to arrive in town late last night," Shayna says.

"Do you think she'll show?" Bryce asks.

Shayna glances toward the door. "I don't know. She said she would if she could, but her messages were a little shorter than usual." She frowns.

Bryce rolls her eyes. "Guess it depends if Miles lets her off the leash. He does realize he's only her brother?"

"Miles is…" Amara asks.

"Oh yeah—" Shayna starts, but Bryce interrupts.

"Her overbearing and overprotective brother," Bryce says.

Shayna shakes her head. "He's the safety for the Kingsmen and Lee's best friend," Shayna adds, giving Bryce a look that says she needs to give it a break with the Miles hate for a minute. "Twyla is his sister, and she comes for visits a lot. She's engaged."

"Got it," Amara says with a nod and reaches for her wine.

"You seem concerned," I say to Shayna.

She rocks her head back and forth. "She's seemed… off or something lately. Not her usual happy self."

I frown. Not because I know Twyla, but probably more because it reminds me of myself last year. I'm sure if she's engaged, she's happy, but for me, my relationship changed me. I never want to be that person again.

"Hopefully she'll come join the fun." Amara raises her

glass and takes a generous sip. "How are things going at Brady's?"

"Yes, do tell." Bryce waggles her eyebrows.

I pick up my martini glass. "What's that supposed to mean?"

"I feel like I sensed some sexual tension the other day at training camp when he walked up." Bryce eyes me, waiting for my answer. It's plain to see why she's a good reporter. She's direct and observant.

I sip my drink to buy myself some time as I glance at Shayna. Lee knows we slept together, and I have to assume her fiancé has told her, so I don't know if Bryce is asking because she already knows something or if it really is a genuine question. I'm way too new to this group to know.

Shayna gives a subtle shake of her head, which I take means Bryce doesn't know anything and it's up to me whether I want to divulge that information. I might as well. Bryce is the only one at the table who doesn't know. Since she's a reporter, I'm a tad scared to say anything about Brady and me, but Shayna trusts her so I hope I can too.

"Truth is that I hooked up with Brady about six months before I got the job with him," I explain to Bryce, telling her everything that happened—minus our kiss in the pantry the other day.

She twirls her wineglass by the stem. "Well damn. What are you gonna do about it?"

"What do you mean?" I pull the stick holding the olive from my drink.

"There's obviously still sexual tension between you two. That kinda thing doesn't just go away, trust me." The corners of Bryce's lips tilt down. "I wish it did."

Shayna's head whips in her direction. "What's that mean? Who are you referring to?"

"Nothing. I'm just saying… it's going to keep building and building until something happens. It's inevitable."

"It's not inevitable," I insist, then bite the olive off the stick.

Bryce shrugs. "If you say so."

"Brady and Bryce almost had a thing," Shayna blurts. We're on our second drink by now and I think she might be feeling it.

"You did?" I look at Bryce, my stomach in knots with jealousy. She's gorgeous and definitely more the type I figured he would prefer.

She rolls her eyes. "We did not almost have a thing. We flirted a little one night, like, a year ago when we first met at a club. It wasn't a big deal."

I believe her, but still, jealousy sours my stomach. My throat closes and I choke on the olive. Amara pats my back and I sip my drink to get it down.

"Did he try to get you to go home with him?" Amara asks.

Bryce shakes her head. "Not at all. We moved pretty quickly from flirting to friendly conversation—I swear." She holds her hands up in front of her, giving Shayla a sour look.

Trying to play it off, I shrug. "It's none of my business or my concern."

Bryce chuckles. "Yeah, right. I was afraid you were going to launch yourself over the table and strangle me."

I sigh because she's right. I have no right to my reaction, but it is what it is, nonetheless.

"See. Told you. Something's gonna happen." Bryce looks smug, and I can't say she shouldn't. Especially after tonight when Brady saw me in this dress.

I crumple under the weight of stares. "It already has." My hands fly up to cover my face.

A collective gasp goes around the table.

Amara gently pulls my hands from my face. "What happened?"

"The other day I was having trouble getting the oatmeal off the top shelf of the pantry and he came in to help and one thing led to another and we ended up making out." I glance at Shayna. "It was right before Lee knocked on the door to pick him up for training camp."

She nods as though she's had a feeling all along.

"What happened afterward?" Amara asks, concern in her voice—probably because she knows how not like me this is.

"Nothing at first. He brought it up later, and we agreed that it couldn't happen again and we'd be best to try to act like it never happened."

Bryce scoffs. "Good luck with that."

"You've never hooked up with someone before and acted like it didn't happen?" Shayna arches a brow at her.

She waves her off. "We're not talking about me."

"So what are you going to do?" Amara asks.

My hands fly up from my sides. "I have no idea. It's so hard, you guys. He's sooo hot, and he's the best father and he actually seems like a nice guy... you should have seen the way he was looking at me before I left tonight."

"I'll bet. That dress is hot as hell on you." Bryce brings her wineglass to her lips.

"Still. Nothing can happen again."

"And why is that exactly?" Shayna asks.

I'm surprised she's the one asking. With the little I know about these two, it wouldn't surprise me if Bryce told me to go for it, but Shayna seems more practical and levelheaded.

I tick off all the reasons on my fingers. "Because he's my boss. Because it would make things complicated. Because we'd have to hide it from Theo. What if it fizzled out quickly and then I still have months left of living and working with him?"

I don't list my last reason. Amara is the only other person in the world who knows about it, and I don't want to go digging up that particular mistake of mine tonight. But she must know it's on my mind because she squeezes my knee.

Shayna shrugs. "I worked with Lee when we started

hooking up. That all worked out. Even before I got my job back with the team, he was worth it in the end."

"You guys are supposed to be telling me what a horrible idea this is, not trying to convince me to sleep with my boss." I toss back the rest of my martini and flag down the waitress, motioning for her to bring me another one.

"You're not going to be working for him forever, are you?" Bryce also motions to the waitress for another drink.

"No, just until Theo's mom comes back in another couple of months."

"Then what's the problem? Get things going now and keep them going once you're not working for him." Bryce shrugs as if it's that easy.

"Do you not want a relationship with Brady?" Shayna asks.

I glance at Amara, knowing that if I have to explain why that might be the case, I'll have to open up about my ex... and potentially the rest of my history with men.

Before I can answer, a pretty, petite woman with long, dark curls approaches us.

"Twyla! You made it!" Shayna jumps out of her seat and envelops her in a hug, then looks at Amara and me. "This is Miles's sister, Twyla. Twyla, this is Amara and Violet. Violet's Theo's nanny."

"Hi," she says in a shaky voice and raises her hand in a halfhearted wave.

Shayna's forehead wrinkles and she yanks Twyla's left hand toward her. "Wait. Where's your engagement ring?"

Twyla bursts into tears, covering her face with her hands. I feel horrible about this girl's pain, but at the same time, I'm thankful to be out of the hot seat.

"Oh my god, what's going on?" Shayna pulls out the chair at the end of the table and gently helps her sit.

I glance at Amara. I'm not sure what to do. Should we

leave these three alone, the two women closest to console Twyla?

"Whose ass do I need to kick?" Bryce asks, and I'm pretty sure she's not kidding. She's clearly a ride-or-die kinda girl. She flags down the waitress. "Round of Patrón, please." Her finger whirls around the table.

"Mathew called off the wedding. He said he met someone else." More tears streak down Twyla's face and my heart squeezes for this poor woman.

"That bastard!" Bryce shouts, getting the attention of some guys at the next table over. She waves. "Turn back around."

"Oh, honey, I'm so sorry." Shayna rubs her back.

"Can you believe that he's ditching me for someone he finds more interesting? He shouldn't be interested in anyone other than me, his fiancée!" Her voice picks up and she's moving into the anger stage quicker than I did.

"Were you together for a long time?" I ask.

She nods. "Since college. We've been engaged for almost a year. The wedding is all planned for October." She wipes the tears with the back of her hand, not bothering to blot them with the drink napkins.

"What a piece of shit," Bryce mumbles.

"He broke it off a few days ago. I wasn't even going to come on this trip, but I figured a few days away would be good. Everyone I know there looks at me with pity and I just want to scream."

The waitress comes over and sets down the shots. "Can I get you anything else?" she asks Twyla a little warily, given her current state.

She downs the shot and says, "Yeah, another shot of tequila and a spiked Arnold Palmer please."

"Anything you want." The waitress nods and heads toward the bar.

"What did Miles say?" Shayna asks, giving Bryce a warning stare to keep her mouth shut about him.

Twyla rolls her eyes. "A whole lot of 'I told you sos' and a big lecture about how I can do better." She sniffles.

"Jackass," Bryce mumbles.

Shayna glares at Bryce with annoyance.

Twyla turns to Bryce. "Right? I swear, all men are idiots."

"Is there any chance of reconciliation?" Amara asks.

Twyla shakes her head. "He told me that all the pressure from the wedding was getting to him and it was my fault because I was making such a big deal about one day in our lives." She flails her arms. "Like, forgive me for wanting our big day to be something really special."

"Well, I don't know him, but he sounds like a jerk. You're probably better off without him." I squeeze her hand, overwhelmed with empathy.

"Cheers to that." Bryce raises her shot glass and downs it.

"Yeah, Vi would know better than anyone," Amara says.

I turn my head in her direction and glare. Her eyes widen and she covers her mouth with her hand, briefly mouthing "sorry."

"What's that mean?" Bryce's head tilts as if her little reporter antennae went up.

I might as well tell them at this point. I'm sure they've all had bad relationships. Huffing out a sigh, I say, "I broke off my engagement last year. I found him cheating on me, so I ended it."

"Oh wow, I'm so sorry." Twyla's jaw hangs open, which is really sweet of her given her current circumstances.

"God, men really suck, don't they?" Bryce sips her drink.

"Not all men," Shayna mumbles and her cheeks flare. I get her sticking up for Lee. Whatever they have together must be special because I'd die for someone to look at me like he does her.

"How did you deal with it?" Twyla asks, her big eyes looking at me as though I hold the answers that will put the pieces of her heart back together.

I laugh, although it's not funny. "I had to move back in with my parents—which was traumatizing in and of itself—and I was really sad for about six months. Then one day, I decided I needed to move on with my life. At first it was hard, but as time went by, I was able to find happiness in things I used to. I think time is your best friend." I cover my hand with hers.

"That's when she slept with Brady. As part of her rebound attempt," Amara says and quickly takes a sip of her wine. After swallowing, she swears to herself. "I don't know what's with my loose lips tonight."

Twyla's eyes go wide and her eyebrows shoot up. "Wait. You slept with Brady Banks?"

"Never mind that right now. What's important is that you know that you'll get through this, and you'll be happy again. It just might take a while." I pat her hand while giving Amara a scathing look.

She sinks into her chair and sips her wine, looking as guilty—as she should.

Twyla frowns and nods, squeezing my hand. "Thanks, I actually feel a little better talking with someone who's gone through something similar and come out the other side. I hope I come out looking as good as you." She motions to my dress.

"I'll bet you come out looking even better." I wink.

The whole table laughs, and we spend the rest of the night listening to Twyla shit talk her ex.

By the time we're ready to go home, I leave the bar feeling raw and vulnerable, much like I did the night I first met Brady.

fifteen

· · ·

Brady

"Fuck!" I toss the pillow under my head across the room and stare at the dark ceiling.

I don't know why the hell I can't sleep. My mind wanders to thoughts of Violet and wanting to make sure she gets home okay, but I don't even know why I'm worried. She's a grown-ass woman who had been out plenty of times before I was even in her life. She can handle herself. I've been on edge all night, wondering what she's doing, who she's talking to. If it's a dickhead she's talking to. I ignore the part of my brain that tells me it's because I want to make sure she actually comes home… er… here and doesn't go home with some other guy tonight.

Why shouldn't she? She's single. She can mess around with whomever she wants.

But the thought of someone else's hands on her makes me want to crush something. The feeling roaring inside me is completely unfamiliar and unwelcome.

I grab the pillow in the middle of my king-size bed and pull it under my head, turning over to my side and closing my eyes. But sleep never comes. Jesus, this is so frustrating. Not one bit of me is tired right now. Quite the opposite actually. I'm all wired up and should probably use my hand to relieve the tension.

Violet was stunning tonight. The thin black leather tucked to her body like cling wrap, and though I'm not into it, it kind of made me want to see her in a dominatrix outfit. Or maybe Catwoman. A whip? Hmm… possibly. Shit, I've seriously lost it now.

The sound of something downstairs makes me sit up. I listen and hear the noise again, so I climb out of bed, wearing only my gray boxer briefs, and open my bedroom door a sliver.

I hear Violet's voice and breathe a sigh of relief. Good, she's home.

But then I hear someone else's voice and I straighten. It's all the way downstairs, so I can't make out whether it's male or female, but someone else is definitely down there.

Did one of her friends come back here with her to continue the party? That doesn't really seem like Violet. Neither does bringing a hookup here, but still that fear worries me.

Every muscle in my body goes rigid. And not just because I'd be pissed if any nanny brought a guy home with her, but because the idea of Violet taking some douchebag to bed across the hall from me sets fire to my blood and sends it scalding through my veins.

I start toward the stairs without thinking twice, rushing down them and into the kitchen where I hear her, or them, rustling around. When I walk in, I see that just the under-counter lights are on, but no one is there. Then I notice the pantry door is open.

"Shit," Violet whispers.

If she's making out with someone else in there, I am going to lose my shit because that's our fucking place.

Do you even hear yourself, Banks?

I stomp over and flick on the light.

"Oh Jesus." She brings her hand up to shield her eyes.

I glance around and see that it's just her in the small space, so I turn the light back off. "I thought I heard someone else."

"Oh sorry, I just called Amara to let her know I got home okay. I hit the speaker button by accident." She giggles. She's definitely feeling good from however many drinks she put down tonight.

"I thought you brought someone home with you." My voice is more rigid than I intend.

"Why would I—oh, wait. Like a guy? To hook up with?" She grabs the box of Cheez-Its and digs her hand in, pulling out a few and eating them. With the dim light from the kitchen, I can make out that her face has transitioned into a scowl. "Are you serious?"

"How the hell am I supposed to know?" My hands fist at my sides.

"Um… maybe because you know me, and I would never do that. Jesus, Brady." She pulls out a few more cheese squares and pops them in her mouth.

I step closer to her. "It's not something we ever discussed as being okay or not."

She takes steps to meet me, and because she still has her heels on, she's closer than normal to lining up to my lips. "I wouldn't think we'd have to have that discussion. It should be implied. I would never bring a guy back to your house to hook up with." She puts the box on the counter and tilts her head in a sassy way.

I shrug. "Why not? You're single. You're free to do what you want." I don't know why I'm taunting her.

"That's right, I am. But if I wanted to hook up with some-one, I would have gone back to his place, not brought a stranger to my boss's house."

The sound that comes out of me can best be described as a growl. Instead of sending Violet running, quite the opposite happens.

She takes another step toward me. "You have something to say about that?"

She smirks. Although I should turn and walk away, a bigger part of me wants to kiss that smug look off her face. Without warning her, I wrap my arm around her waist, pulling her into me, bend my head, and kiss her.

She practically melts in my arms, moaning and wrapping her arms around my neck. Our tongues meet, and the sensation of our connection sends lightning bolts through my body. My cock hardens, and I can't help but angle my hips into her. Her arms come down from around my neck and roam my bare chest as though she can't get enough. I forgot what it was like to have her palms coast over my hard body, and I vow never to forget again.

I pull away and push my hands into her hair at her temples. "How much have you had to drink tonight?"

"Not so much that I can't make this decision for myself."

She pulls me back to her, smashing my lips back down on hers. My hands grip her ass cheeks and I thrust my cock into her abdomen. We both groan at the sensation, and I want to hear more of that from her. In fact, I want to hear her call out my name when she comes from my dick deep in her wetness.

I force her to walk backward until her back hits the pantry shelving, then I pull away from the kiss and stare into her dark hooded eyes while I slowly pull her leg all the way up so that the back of her thigh rests on my chest. She's essentially doing a split standing up, but I know from our night together that she's more than capable.

She meets my gaze, never glancing away, never telling me to stop. She's perfect.

"You good?" I check in with her.

Violet bites her bottom lip and nods.

Starting at her ankle, I lazily let my fingers coast down her calf and under the sensitive spot behind her knee, all the way up her inner thigh until I reach her center. One swipe of my knuckle and I groan because her panties are already soaked.

"Fuck," I murmur, and her lids close when I ghost my finger over the wet silk fabric again. "I wanna watch you come, Violet. It's been too long. Tell me. Do you want to come?"

She nods quickly, biting her bottom lip and looking as though she'll beg for it if she has to.

I bend my head and lean into her ear. "I wanna hear you say it. Tell me you want me to make you come." I circle her clit once with my thumb as my fingers tease the elastic along the sides and she whimpers.

"I want you to make me come. Please, Brady... please make me come."

My cock grows painfully harder, and I smash my lips to hers again. As our tongues meet, I slip the fabric of her panties to the side and my fingers explore the slickness of her pussy. She's hot and wet and so ready for me. I delve through her folds and circle her entrance but don't push inside, causing her to make a needy sound in the back of her throat. I chuckle into our kiss.

When I reach her clit, I circle it with my fingertips until she's a writhing mess. From the amount of pressure her leg is putting on my chest, she wants to close her legs, but I stand firm, holding her open, leaving her at my mercy.

I push two fingers inside her, and she breaks our kiss, throwing her head back, arching into me. I use my thumb to circle her clit as I insert my fingers back inside her wetness. Some other time I'll tease an orgasm out of her slowly. Right now, I want to watch her come apart as hard and as fast as I can make her.

I keep two fingers inside her and place my thumb on her clit, thrusting my fingers in and out without ever removing them. She soaks my fingers and her nails dig into my shoulders as she arches her back and her neck, breathing heavily.

My breathing labors from watching her. I intensify my efforts and move my fingers faster, causing her to cry out and convulse in my arms.

"Oh, Brady—oh my god, Brady!"

Her hips jerk, and I use the hand snaked around her back to keep her body pressed against me. I watch her climax subside until she's like putty in my arms, and I gently take the ankle of her leg that's straight up and bring it back down until her foot is on the floor.

She leans her weight against the pantry shelf and looks more relaxed than I can remember seeing her. Even that night. "That was—wow."

"Would you give me your number now?" I arch an eyebrow. I know beyond a doubt that she enjoyed what we just did.

She chuckles and swats at me lazily. "I told you that's not why I didn't give you my number. You've earned a gold star in the orgasm department."

"You sure about that?"

"Very. Now... should we take care of that?" She gestures to my waist and my hard-on that's desperate to break through the cotton barrier of my boxer briefs. She moves to push off the shelving, but I step back.

"This was all about you, not me." And I mean it.

Not saying I wouldn't love to be pushing into her right now, but we have some shit to sort out first. The last thing I want is for her to regret sleeping with me... again.

She frowns. "You don't want *me* to make you come?"

I groan and push a hand through my hair. This woman has no idea what she does to me with her words. "I do, believe me, I do. But I'm trying to be a decent guy here. I think we should have a conversation about what this means before we go any further."

She makes a face, but she nods. Then she nods a second

time. "Can we talk about this in the morning when I have a clear head? I'm so relaxed right now I just want to go to bed."

I step into her because I can't resist. "Of course we can." I give her a chaste kiss on the lips. Taking her hand, I lead her, clicking heels and all, to the stairs. "Mind if we take those off so they don't wake Theo?" I gesture to her hot-as-hell heels and fishnet socks.

"Not at all." She sits on the third step from the bottom and bends down to take off her shoe.

"Here, let me." I fall to my knee, proceeding to take off each shoe, then I pull off the fishnet socks while she watches me. I swear she sucks in a breath every time my fingers graze her ankle.

"Thanks," she says in a soft voice when I hand her the socks and help her back up.

We walk up the stairs quietly, and I follow her to her bedroom door. When she reaches the doorway, she reaches for her shoes that are still in my hand.

Before I pass them over, I give her another kiss. It's slow and passionate and I hope it conveys all the things I hope to be doing with her soon.

"Sweet dreams, Violet." I take a few backward steps toward my door across the hall.

"Same to you, Brady." She goes into her room and softly closes the door.

I do the same and enter my room, leaning back on the door once it's shut behind me. Hopefully now I can get some sleep, though I suspect that even if I do, I'll be dreaming of the woman across the hall.

sixteen

. . .

Violet

Theo has been begging me to teach him yoga, so Sunday afternoon when Brady returns from training camp, he finds us in the family room practicing downward dog.

I saw him briefly this morning before he left, and I basically ignored his gaze. I know we need to discuss what happened last night, but while being exhausted and slightly hungover early on a Sunday was not the time to have that conversation.

"What's going on here?" He flops onto the couch and I glance at him. He looks more tired than usual. Training camp seems to be taking a lot out of him.

"Violet's showing me how she does her yoga. Want to try, Daddy?" Theo falls out of his pose and lands on his side with a giggle.

"Maybe some other time. I'm pretty wiped from camp today. I'll just watch you guys."

I get out of my pose and straighten up to go over and help Theo try again. "How did it go?" I try to keep my voice light, but images from last night keep flashing through my mind.

Brady blows out a breath. "Good, I guess. I'm glad it's a

shorter day than normal at least. Found I was pretty distracted through most of it though."

I look his way as I try to show Theo how to keep his heels pressed to the floor. "Oh? Why's that?"

He shrugs but gives me a look I swear could incinerate me. "Just had some things running through my mind. *Someone.*"

I swallow hard. "Gotcha."

Theo falls out of pose again and rolls over to look up at me from the floor. "This is hard."

"You're doing great. It takes practice." I smile at him.

"Can I go do my Lego set in my room now?" This kid and his Lego addiction, I swear. He always has one set going here in the family room and one in his room.

"Of course. Want me to come help?"

He sits up and shakes his head. "No, I wanna try to do this one by myself."

A part of me wants to beg him to let me come with him so that I won't be forced to be alone with Brady, knowing he'll likely use this opportunity to have the conversation I don't want to have. But it's time to put on my big girl panties. Bryce was right when she said something was going to happen. And if I thought that the sexual tension between us would dissipate because he gave me an earth-shattering orgasm last night, I was sorely mistaken.

In fact, the way he's looking at me now makes me feel as though he wants me more than ever and I'd be lying if I said the same wasn't true on my end.

I ruffle Theo's hair. "All right. I'll come check on you in a bit and see if you've changed your mind."

Unexpectedly, Theo jolts forward and encompasses me in a hug, wrapping his arms around my waist. "Thanks for showing me yoga."

Slowly, I let my arms come around him and squeeze him back. "You're welcome."

I always love the kids I work with, and I always want them to feel that, but there's something special about my relationship with Theo that's different than any of the other kids I've cared for. I'm going to miss this little guy so much in a couple of months when it's time for me to move on.

I glance up while Theo's in my arms and see this expression on Brady's face that I can't place. It's a little like awe mixed with apprehension and I don't know what to make of it.

Theo rushes off without a clue about the strange vibe in the room.

"I'm going to go change out of these yoga clothes," I say.

When Theo insisted I show him some poses, I changed into my leggings and a tank with a built-in bra since I didn't want the T-shirt I'd been wearing riding up or falling down over my head when I was leaning over. That little guy doesn't need to know what my bras look like even if his father does.

I'm a few steps away from where I was when Brady calls, "Wait."

I briefly close my eyes but turn and put on a brave face. "Yeah?"

I know we need to have this conversation, I do, but I also know that everything will change afterward—for the worse or for the better, I'm not sure.

He stands from the couch and walks over to stand in front of me. "We need to talk about what happened last night." His eyes search my face, which I can feel heating.

"Yeah, we probably should." I want him to start so I know where his head is.

He winces and grips the back of his neck with one hand. "If I made you uncomfortable or if you feel like I took advantage of you in any way, I'm sor—"

I shake my head. "Brady, you didn't take advantage of me."

"But you'd been drinking."

I rest a hand on his shoulder. "I wasn't that drunk. I knew exactly what I was doing. I was just as into it as you."

His muscle flexes under my palm and I drop my hand, suddenly aware of the heat from his skin beneath the thin cotton fabric of his shirt.

"Are you sure? Would you even tell me if you did feel pressured? I'm essentially your boss." The hand at the back of his neck drops to his side and he looks at me with worried eyes.

"What we had started well before you were my boss. I would think it's obvious from our night together that I'm attracted to you."

Images of that night flash in front of my eyes and I think it must be the same for him too because his lids grow heavy.

"You'd tell me if I made you uncomfortable?" He arches an eyebrow.

"Absolutely. I really would." I nod, and that seems to settle him because his shoulders relax.

We're silent for a bit, then he says, "I suppose this is the part of the conversation where we have to figure out how we want to move forward. So, do you want what happened last night to happen again?"

I can't say the words, so I simply nod once. It's scary to admit, but at the same time, I no longer feel as though I have an anvil on my head, weighing me down, now that the truth is out there.

His nostrils flare. "So do I." Brady looks over his shoulder at the entry to the room and then steps toward me, resting his hands on my hips. "I have all kinds of ideas about what else we can do. In fact, it's all I could think about today." He leans in and whispers in my ear, "I fumbled twice today just thinking about tasting your pussy again."

His dirty words and the image of his head between my legs causes me to stop breathing for a beat. When I recover, I pull back and meet his gaze. "I like the way your mind works."

He grins. "Good, because there's a lot more."

I swallow hard. "This has to stay between us though. No one can know, especially Theo."

He nods. "We're on the same page. I don't want to confuse him."

His comment stings because it makes it clear that whatever arrangement we're negotiating here isn't a relationship. But he brings up a good point and one that we should agree upon now.

"I don't either, and I don't want either of us to be confused." His forehead creases as though he doesn't know where I'm going with this. "This... thing between us isn't serious. And it ends when I leave here. I want to make sure we're on the same page about that."

His gaze skirts over my face, looking for what, I can't be sure, but he nods. "Okay."

I don't know if I expected or wanted him to argue with me, but his one-word answer leaves me disappointed even though I'm the one who brought it up.

"Now that we've sorted all that out, can I please kiss you?"

I glance behind him at the doorway. Since we're free and clear, I nod.

He brings his lips to mine, his tongue coasting over my lips until I open for him and we sink into each other. My nipples tighten in my bra and my core aches for more of what he gave me last night.

This. This feeling right here is why we're doing this. I'm going to enjoy it for the next couple of months, then I'll move on with my life and he'll move on with his.

Brady Banks will just be a memory. Best-laid plans.

seventeen

. . .

Brady

The night of our talk, I don't initiate anything with Violet. For one, I'm beyond exhausted after being up half the night and then being drilled at training camp all day. And two, I want to let the idea of what we agreed to sit with her for at least twenty-four hours before I try anything in case she changes her mind.

No matter what she says, we're in a tricky situation since she works for me, and I want to be sure she doesn't feel pressured to embark on a sexual relationship with me.

Even though we agreed this is casual, I don't want Violet to feel like a booty call, so I give a lot of thought to how I want to initiate sex with her. It can't be superromantic, but I want her to feel desired, so I decide that some wine on the balcony after Theo's gone to bed will be a nice relaxing setting.

It's warm out tonight, but I bring up a blanket anyway in case she gets cold, set the wine bottle and glasses on the table that rests in front of the outdoor couch and chairs, and turn on some light jazz on the outdoor speakers. Mood set.

I head down to the second level and find her where I

expected—in her bedroom, reading in the chair in the corner. The door is open, so I knock softly and step inside.

Violet looks up from her book. "Hey."

"Mind if I interrupt you?"

She shifts in her chair and sets the book aside. "Of course not. What's up?"

Am I imagining the anticipatory glint in her eyes?

"Wanted to see if you want to share a bottle of wine with me up on the balcony?" I thumb behind me.

Her smile lights up the room. "I'd love to." She walks over to me.

My hand slides down her arm, and I entwine our fingers, leading her to the next level. I gesture for her to sit on the couch. I pour us each a glass of red wine and hand her hers before I sit to her left.

"This view is gorgeous. I haven't been up here at night yet."

I look out over the city and all its sparkling lights, then at the Golden Gate Bridge in the distance, lit up and glowing red in the dark.

"I like to sit up here when the weather is nice. It's relaxing." I bring my wineglass to my lips.

My nutritionist would not be happy to know I'm drinking tonight, but what he doesn't know won't hurt him. It's not like I could invite Violet up to drink on her own. Sacrifices must be made.

"I can see why. If this was my house, I'd be up here every night. Even when it's cold."

I chuckle, but I'm a little unsettled when I realize how much I like the idea of her feeling like this is her home. "Theo told me you took him to the Children's Creativity Museum today."

Her eyes sparkle when she shifts to look at me and not the view. "You should have seen him. He loved interacting with everything and was smiling and laughing the whole time. He's so smart, Brady."

The expression on her face when she talks about my son reminds me of Hannah's or my mom's or the twins— someone who loves and cares for him. I couldn't ask for a better person to watch over my son when I'm not around. She treats him as if he's her own.

"I might be biased, but I agree."

Violet looks at me thoughtfully for a beat and I wonder what's going through that mind of hers.

"Can I ask you something?" She sounds a little nervous.

"Go for it." I sip my wine.

"Has Theo ever known you and Hannah as a couple? I know you said you hadn't been one for a while, but I didn't know what that meant. If she found out... about us, I can't help but wonder what she'll think."

I don't know why, but it irks me that she's once again concerned about the status of my and Hannah's relationship. I already told her there's nothing to worry about.

"Theo's never known us as a couple. We tried to give it a go when she found out she was pregnant but realized it wasn't going to work shortly after Theo was born, so he's only ever known us apart." I tear my gaze away from her and to the view.

"That upsets you."

I turn to look back at her. "Not in the way you might think. I grew up without a mom until I was around Theo's age, so I remember what that was like. He has a mom, of course, and she's a great one, but I always swore I wanted to give my kid a nuclear family. I wanted him to grow up in a household with a mom and a dad, but it is what it is." I shrug. "I wouldn't change anything if it meant not having him in my life."

"Makes sense." She nods slowly before taking a sip of her wine.

"I still want that for him. For me." I meet her gaze, but this time it's her who dodges eye contact and uses the view as an excuse to look away.

"He really misses his mom."

I frown. "Yeah, I know. It's great that he video chats with her all the time, but it's not the same."

"He keeps asking me how many days it is until she comes home."

I've noticed the longer Hannah's been gone, the more Theo asks about her returning. I thought it would be easier as time went on, but it's becoming harder.

I clear my throat to change the subject. "Speaking of Theo, I need to get on planning his sixth birthday party. It's coming up in a few weeks. Usually Hannah does most of that stuff, but with her gone, I need to take care of it."

She turns to look at me, eyes brimming with excitement. "I'm happy to help."

I shake my head. "I can't ask you to do that."

Her head tilts. "Brady, I want to. He's an amazing kid. It's no trouble."

I eye her skeptically. "Are you sure?"

"Absolutely! I can grab the decorations and order a cake. Is there a theme you had in mind?"

We both laugh and say at the same time, "Lego."

I could kiss her for offering to help me. I could probably muddle my way through, but Theo's party will be in better hands with Violet at the helm rather than me.

"You take care of the guest list and I'll handle the rest. How does that sound?"

"Like you're an angel." I push the hand not holding the wineglass into her hair, pulling her toward me until our lips meet. When my tongue brushes against hers, I sigh in relief. It hasn't been that long, but it feels as if it's been ages since I've tasted her. Then my phone dings on the table, and I groan and pull away. "I just want to make sure that's not Theo leaving his room."

Since this house is so big, I have an app that alerts me if his bedroom door opens after I've put him to bed for the night.

"It's just Miles ranting—again." I set the phone back down with a shake of my head.

"Everything okay?" She sips her wine.

"Yeah, the guys and I have spent the entire week trying to convince him not to fly east and beat the shit out of his sister's ex-fiancé. Did Twyla tell you what happened when you met her this weekend?"

"Yeah, she did."

Something in her voice catches my attention. I tilt my head. "The guy is clearly a loser. Miles never liked him."

She nods and looks at the lights that sparkle below.

"What is it?" I take her hand that's not holding her wineglass.

Violet sighs. "Just brings back memories, that's all."

"Of Saturday?" My forehead wrinkles.

"No. Of when I felt the same way Twyla does right now." She turns her head to look at me, and there's a deep sadness in her eyes. It makes me want to pummel whoever is responsible for putting it there.

"What happened?" I squeeze her hand.

"My fiancé cheated on me."

I still. I think I even stop breathing for a beat. "You were engaged?"

Violet nods. "Yeah, then I found out he was cheating on me, so I ended it. That was about six months before I first met you." She bites her bottom lip for a moment, as though she has something she needs to say but doesn't want to.

"What? What is it?" My heart races. Is she going to tell me they're still involved, she still has feelings for him, what?

"The night we met was my attempt at a rebound. One-night stands aren't really my thing, but I was trying to forget about him and move on with my life and that's why I went to the hotel with you." She says the last bit really fast as if maybe I won't catch it.

Understanding dawns on me. "That's why you wouldn't give me your number."

Could that be why she was so adamant that this thing between us remain casual even now?

She nods and cringes. "Are you mad?"

"Why would I be mad?"

"I was using you," she says as though it's obvious.

I can't help but laugh. "Violet, I don't care why or how we met, just that we did." I squeeze her hand. "Is that why you wouldn't tell me why you wouldn't give me your number?"

"I thought you might be mad or insulted. Plus, then I'd have to get into my whole failed engagement and that's something I'd rather leave in the past." Her shoulders slump a bit. It clearly still affects her. Whether it's because she still has feelings for the piece of shit or just because it sucks to be cheated on, I can't be sure.

"Let me make one thing clear." I lower my chin so I'm looking directly into her eyes. "That man was an idiot. If he had you locked down for life, he was a complete moron to fuck that up." I hold her gaze so she knows I mean it.

I probably shouldn't have said it—it certainly doesn't make this thing between us feel casual—but she needs to know her worth. Hell, I want to show her her worth.

I take the wineglass from her hand and set it on the table, along with my own. Then I drag her over so that she's straddling me on the couch. My hands drag up the sides of her body, moving to her chest over her cotton-covered breasts and up her neck until I grip her head, forcing her down so I can kiss her.

The moment our tongues meet, our bodies move in rhythm—she rocks her hips while I thrust up into her so that we're dry-humping like teenagers. My hands shift into her hair and she moans, bringing her hands up to grip my wrists as though she's afraid I'll pull away. What started as a small flame ignites into a full-blown forest fire between us as we pant and nip and moan, neither of us fully satisfied.

I pull away from her, and with a cocky grin, I say, "Feel like being naughty?"

Her smile tells me we're on the exact same wavelength.

eighteen

· · ·

Violet

"Feel like being naughty?" The gleam in his hazel eyes only promises the greatest reward for being bad, so I slowly smile wide. "Tell me you're on the pill."

"I am, and I'm clean."

"Me too. Just got tested."

He goes back to kissing me, but one hand travels down over my breast and straight down to cup my sex over the slightly oversized cotton shorts I'm wearing. I can't help but rock against his hand, hoping for more of the friction I seek.

Brady's mouth dips to my neck and he mumbles against my skin, "You have no idea how much I've wanted this pussy since the last time I fucked it."

His words soak my panties and I hum in approval.

With little effort, he draws the crotch of my shorts to the side, along with my panties, and drags his fingers through my slick folds. A huff of air leaves me, and I grip his hair as his mouth travels to bite my nipples over my cotton T-shirt and bra. Then his hands leave my body, and he works the waistband of his athletic shorts until his cock pops out. He situates the elastic waist under his balls, gripping the base and tugging the rigid length a few times.

My insides clench, wanting nothing more than to feel him inside me, coaxing me toward a climax.

"Someone might see us." It's a halfhearted argument. There's no real concern in my voice.

"Maybe. Does that worry you?" He looks absolutely wicked when he asks me, and my nipples harden further inside my bra.

"A little, but I think it turns me on even more." Without further discussion, I position myself over him.

He uses one hand to hold my shorts and underwear to the side and the other to line himself up until I'm sinking down on his length. A small cry leaves my lips and I pause, fully seated with him inside me, stretching me as our eyes meet. His hazel ones look like whiskey in a glass and grow darker as I start moving.

Neither of us diverts our gaze as he slides in and out of me, and I pick up the pace. I lean in, pressing my forehead and nose against his, but we don't kiss. We just breathe each other in over and over again.

There's something erotic about the fact that we're clothed, but our bodies are still joined. If a neighbor or someone from below saw us, they could probably guess what we're doing from the rhythm of our bodies, but they can't *see* anything. Still, Brady and I feel *everything*.

My pace increases as my orgasm barrels toward me like a runaway train. I roll my hips, giving me the friction I need to get there, and Brady brings his hands up to pinch my nipples through my shirt and bra. It's a dull pain and I arch my back, moaning.

"That's it, take it, Violet. Take it all for yourself."

His words, along with the thumb he now has pressed between us, send the runaway train off the tracks at the edge of the cliff and I free-fall into bliss. My body jerks and my fingertips push into the firm muscles of his shoulders. When I come out of the dreamlike state and meet his eyes, they remind me of a wolf's—hungry and on the hunt.

Brady wastes no time, moving his hands to my hips and forcing me to stay there while he pummels into me from below. I take it, basking in the euphoric sensation of his cock drilling in and out of me, lighting every nerve ending on fire in the best possible way. He's like a man possessed and cries out my name when he comes inside me.

Neither of us moves while we catch our breaths. When he does eventually pull out of me, I feel the evidence of his climax between my thighs as I slip off him to the side.

"Hang on a second." He tucks his glistening length back in his shorts and rushes toward the door that leads inside.

I stare up at the night sky, reliving what we just did. Not only does Brady make me feel amazing, but when I'm with him, I'm solely focused on him and the way he makes my body sing. I get out of my head and all the stuff that runs through my brain all day long.

"Let's clean you up."

I didn't even notice that he'd returned, and he's bending with a wet cloth to clean me up.

"I can do it." When I hold out my hand, he passes me the cloth.

He watches as I tilt onto my back and slide the cloth past the waistband of my shorts to wipe myself off. When I'm done, he takes it from me and tosses it on the table, then takes a seat in the corner of the couch.

"Come here." He motions for me to move closer to him, so I do and he tucks me under his arm.

I must drift off at some point because I wake up later in my bed, not remembering how I got there. The idea of Brady carrying me to bed causes a warm feeling to radiate outward from my chest, but I do my best to pretend it's not there, rolling over to fall back asleep.

It's not a good sign when I wake in the morning and that feeling is still there.

———

The next morning when Brady appears in the kitchen while I'm making coffee, I'm not sure how to react. Will things be weird between us now that we've slept together again? Did he enjoy himself as much as he says he did before? Are we going to talk about it or pretend like it never happened at all?

But I don't have to wonder long because seconds after he walks into the kitchen, he says good morning and reaches for my waist from behind and turns me to face him.

"Morning," I say with what probably looks like a worshiping smile.

He leans in to give me what I think will be a quick, chaste kiss, but instead his tongue licks along the seam of my lips and I open for him.

Good thing I already brushed my teeth.

"I've been thinking of you since I got up." He slides his hands down from my waist to my ass.

I can't help the cheesy grin that appears on my face. "Is that so?"

He nods slowly. "C'mon."

He takes my hand and leads me to the pantry.

"What are you doing?"

He flicks on the light once we're inside and closes the door. "I need to reacquaint myself with the taste of your pussy. I can't stop thinking about it after last night."

My eyes practically bulge out of my head. "Don't you have to get to training camp?"

He takes a quick glance at his Apple watch. "I have five minutes. I can make you come in five minutes."

My insides quake at his promise. He'll probably get me there in three.

Without another word, he slides my shorts and underwear to the floor, picks me up by the waist, and deposits me on the counter that runs along the back of the pantry. My breath comes out in short spurts of shallow air, anticipating his face between my legs. He spreads my legs up in a V, holding my calves, then bends down and licks me from my entrance to my clit.

My head flops back against the wall on a moan and I grip the edge of the counter to keep my balance. "Holy shit, Brady."

Brady is like a man starved, licking and sucking and fucking me with his tongue. My core tightens more and more with his attention and my fingers are white as they grip the edge of the counter. I'm biting my lip so hard not to moan because there's no way I want to be interrupted right now.

When I'm close to coming, my legs start to close of their own accord, but Brady shakes his head and forces them wide with his palms, keeping me open. With one final hard pull on my clit with his mouth, a loud moan is wrenched from my throat, and I come hard and fast. A rolling tide of sensation crashes through my body as he laps me up.

Without a word, Brady lowers my legs, gently takes my waist, pulls me from the counter, and sets me on my feet. Once he's sure I can stand, he bends to retrieve my under-wear and shorts and gently pulls them up my legs.

It's such a juxtaposition from the man who just ate me with abandon.

With a cocky grin, he glances at his watch. "One minute to spare." Then he grips the back of my neck and kisses me so that I can taste myself on his tongue before he pulls away and rests his forehead on mine. "I'll see you and that pussy tonight."

I nod numbly, still overwhelmed by what just happened.

And then he's gone and I'm left standing in the pantry by

myself, wondering if the next couple of months will be like this, and if so, how the hell am I ever going to give him up when it's time for me to leave?

nineteen

· · ·

Brady

The last eighteen hours with Violet have been beyond my expectations. I knew we were good together, but fuck me, it's even more potent than I remembered. I don't know if that's because I know her better now, but when we're together, it feels as though nothing else matters, as though nothing could ever be better than the two of us.

She's been on my mind all day, and it's shown. I wasn't at my best today on the field. I'm not worried about my position on the team, but I owe it to my parents and the rest of my teammates to put forth my best effort out there.

"Earth to Brady. What the fuck, man? You've been distracted all day," Chase grumbles.

He, Miles, Lee, and I are all at the training facility, eating the lunch provided by the nutritionists.

"I'm listening, I'm listening," I say.

"Oh yeah? What did I just say?" Miles asks before taking a big bite of his protein bowl.

"I don't know. Probably bitching about your sister's love life again." I arch an eyebrow because, man... I know Miles is an overprotective brother, but he will not let this thing with Twyla go.

Lee laughs and then shrugs. "He's got you there."

"Fuck off." Miles tosses a crumpled-up napkin at Lee. "He dumped my sister for another woman. How do you expect me not to be pissed about that?"

Chase's jaw clenches and the plastic drink bottle he's holding creaks under his grip. He looks at me and I widen my eyes, but he offers no explanation for his anger.

"You have every right to be pissed," I say. "But you don't have to make it your whole personality."

Miles stares at me for a beat, then gives me a short nod as if he's saying fair enough.

"So, what's going on with you?" Lee elbows my side.

Violet and I agreed that this would be a secret, but I think the implication was more that it would be a secret from Theo, Hannah, and the rest of my family. I could really use someone to talk to about this. I feel like a pot about to boil over, but the lid is stuck.

"I slept with Violet again," I blurt.

Miles chokes on his broccoli, thumping on his chest and reaching for his drink.

"I fucking knew it." In a rare display of what might count as happiness, Chase grins.

"How did that happen?" Miles asks, now recovered.

"Well, Miles, when a man and a woman really like each other…"

He rolls his eyes.

"Did you mean for it to happen or was it one of those spur-of-the-moment things?" Lee asks, worry set in his wrinkled forehead.

I push away my tray, not in the mood to eat. "When we kissed, it wasn't planned. She was in the pantry trying to get something from a high shelf and I went in to help and one thing led to another."

Miles frowns. "I thought you said you slept with her?"

"I did. Then the next time was the night she was out with

all the girls. I heard something downstairs and went down to investigate and she was in there looking hotter than sin and... stuff happened."

Chase arches an eyebrow.

"You don't need the details."

He scowls at me.

"After that, we talked about what was going on and decided that it was okay if we messed around as long as we kept it on the DL. I don't want to confuse Theo or anything."

Lee's forehead creases. "But what if it turns into something more than just the two of you fooling around? Would you tell Theo then?"

It's a fair question. I've only been with the team for a year, but I've made it clear to the guys that I don't have any type of relationship history. Being serious with Violet would be new territory for me.

"Doesn't matter. She wants things to remain casual, and I agreed. But it's like I can't get enough. I thought that after we'd got together again, I'd feel some type of satiation, but it's only ramped up all my feelings. I want her more now than I ever did. When I saw her this morning, I practically pulled her into the pantry to make her come." I shake my head at how desperate I felt to give her pleasure this morning.

"Sounds like your pantry's getting a lot of action." Miles tosses a cherry tomato into his mouth.

I glare at him. "Not the point."

Chase leans back in his chair and crosses his arms. "What's the fucking problem, man? You're getting laid on the regular now, enjoying it, and she doesn't want to make it a big fucking thing. Doesn't seem like something to cry about."

When he puts it like that, I wonder, *What is my problem*? A year ago, I would've been thrilled to find myself in a situation like this.

"Maybe I'm overthinking things," I grumble.

"Yeah, or maybe you have real feelings for Violet." Lee

throws a cherry tomato at me and it hits me on the forehead. "Too bad it's not heavy enough to knock some sense into you."

I don't like how his words resonate in my chest. There are a number of problems with that scenario.

First, explaining to Hannah that I did, in fact, sleep with the nanny.

Second, convince Violet that what we have should be something more and not just a fling. But how do I do that in good conscience when I don't even know if I'm relationship material? I tried that once with my son's mom and it went to shit.

Third and most important, how do I bring a woman who's clearly hesitant about opening herself up to love again into Theo's life? I can't risk his heart being broken if things don't work out.

"That's not an option, so it doesn't matter either way," I tell Lee. Then in the interest of moving off this topic of conversation, I direct us to another topic I know will shift the focus. "Has Twyla heard from her ex at all since they broke up?"

"This fucking guy. You won't believe it…" Miles starts.

Chase groans and gives me a death glare.

Miles continues to tell us all the latest updates while I do my best to pretend I'm listening. Really, I'm still thinking about Violet and what Lee just said. Could I want more, and if so, what does that look like?

———

I don't arrive home that late, and when I pull onto my street, Violet and Theo are walking hand in hand down the sidewalk, so I pull off to the side and roll down the window.

"Where are you two headed?" I call.

"Hi, Daddy!" Theo lets go of Violet's hand and rushes

over to the passenger side window. "We're going to the park. Want to come?"

My muscles ache and I'm tired from a lack of sleep for the past few nights, but how can I say no when Theo's eyes twinkle with excitement at the prospect of spending time with me? I know the years will fly by and soon I'll be the last person he wants to hang with.

"Sure thing. I'll meet you guys there after I park at home."

"Okay, Daddy!" He rushes back to Violet, who gives me a shy wave before they continue walking toward the park.

Once I've parked at home and run inside to grab a ball cap and sunglasses, I head out to the park. It only takes me a few minutes to walk there, and I find them around the playground. Violet stands off to the side, watching Brady play with Kale and a couple of other boys.

"Hey, you." I stand by her side, and she glances at me.

She chuckles at my hat and sunglasses. "Going incognito?"

I shrug. "It helps cut down on the number of people who recognize me. I don't love it when fans approach me when I'm with Theo."

Violet's smile feels like sunshine on my face. "That's sweet."

I drop my hand to my side and brush my fingers against hers, not missing her quick intake of air. "How was your day?"

"Good. Hannah called earlier and Theo was a little bummed after, hence why we're here for the second time today." She laughs.

"That's all right. All this fresh air and activity will help him sleep sounder tonight. Then you and I can—" My mind travels to a lot of different scenarios, all with us being naked.

"Daddy, will you push me on the swing?" Theo shouts from the top of the slide.

"Sure, buddy." I turn to face Violet. "If you want to clock

out and head home, I can stay with him until he's had his fill."

She shakes her head. "That's okay. I don't mind."

We walk together over to the swings.

Theo meets us, jumping up on his favorite one. "I wanna go really high, Daddy!"

I start with a gentle shove on his back. "All right. You tell me if it gets to be too much."

With each push from me, Theo goes a little higher until he's giggling and laughing.

"You look like you could fly, Theo!" Violet calls to him.

I glance from her radiant smile to Theo, whose head is thrown back so I can see the look of wonder and excitement on his face, and a strange sensation falls over me.

This feels like a family.

I know how dangerous that thought is, and I hate myself for thinking it because Violet has made it clear that she wants nothing more than a casual hookup. Still, I can't shake how right this thing between us feels.

"Hey, Banks!"

I turn to see one of the dads I recognize.

"Can't wait to see you kick some LA ass next week in preseason." He gives me a thumbs-up and a wave.

"Thanks, man." I return his wave, and he leads his son out of the park.

With his mention of our away game, I make a split-second decision without really thinking it through. "Why don't you come to some of the away games? Usually Theo stays home because Hannah's here, but since she's not, you guys should come. I can get us a suite."

"Yeah, Daddy! That'd be so fun!"

Did I purposely say it in front of Theo, knowing he'd be game? Maybe.

Violet looks from me to Theo, seeming surprised but not put off. "Where's your next away game?

"Where he said." I nod in the direction the guy just went. "Los Angeles."

She bites her bottom lip, and it takes everything in me not to reach for her and drag her into my chest, so I let take her bottom lip with my teeth and tug to free it.

"Okay, that would be fun." Her eyes sparkle with what I think is desire.

"It's definitely going to be fun," I promise.

"Yay!" Theo shouts before jumping off the swing when it's at its highest point.

"Oh my god." Violet's hands fly up to her mouth.

I laugh. "It's all right. He does it all the time."

Her hand goes to her chest. "Not with me he doesn't." She quickly walks to him, but Theo races back to the play structure.

"Guess you bring out his wild side," she says as we follow him.

"He's not the only one." I bump her hip with mine and she laughs.

In this moment, I could listen to that sound forever and die a happy man.

twenty

. . .

Violet

"**I** promise I'll come by next week."

My mother sighs into the phone, then continues the conversation in Korean about how I never make time for her or my father and how I have to make a greater effort. Then she tells me that my brother is thinking of proposing to his longtime girlfriend.

She sounds positively giddy about this development and it makes me realize once again that she never sounds this way when talking about anything to do with my life.

"That's great. I'll be sure to call him and wish him luck." Maybe. "I really have to go though, Mom. We just arrived at the hotel in Los Angeles."

"My friend has a son. He's a surgeon. How about I set you up with him?"

I guffaw. This is a new low for my mom. "No, Umma, I'll find my own man, but thanks."

We say goodbye and I hang up, shoving my phone into my purse, then stare at the swanky hotel we're going to be staying in. I've never stayed anywhere this nice before and probably won't ever again.

"You ready, Theo?"

He nods enthusiastically and we head inside, the suitcase carrying both our things trailing behind.

Brady and the rest of his teammates went straight to the stadium for practice when we landed, and Theo and I took an Uber to the hotel. Brady will meet us here for dinner. We plan to have our meals brought up into the room and watch a movie Theo's been begging to watch.

In the meantime, Theo and I are going to explore the hotel and the surrounding neighborhood, and I promised him we'd go for a swim in the hotel pool. When we looked it up online, we saw that there's a rooftop pool. Apparently, there's nothing more fun than staying in a hotel for a kid. Even for a kid like Theo, who lives in a mini-mansion.

I check us in and leave a key for Brady with the front desk, then Theo and I head up to check out the room. When I push open the door, Theo rushes in ahead of me, and I have to hold in a gasp. It's exquisite.

The large combination living/dining room is surrounded by windows and even has a fireplace separating the spaces. To the right, I spot a doorway that leads to one bedroom, and on the other side of the spacious room are two more doors I imagine lead to the other two bedrooms in the suite. When I roll the suitcase in and let the door close behind me, I see a hallway near one of the bedroom doors that leads to a small kitchenette and powder room.

Everything is decorated in chic California designs with lots of creams, beiges, and light grays. It's spectacular and the nicest place I've ever stayed.

"What do you think of the suite, buddy?"

Theo whips around and grins at me. "It's amazing! Can I pick my room?"

I shrug. "I don't see why not. They're probably all pretty much the same."

He runs to the room on the opposite side that's on its own,

then races past me to check out the other two before running back over to stand in front of me.

"What did you decide?"

He points at the room on the right of the two that are set together. "I want that one. It has blue pillows and blue is my favorite color."

I nod. "Fair enough. Let's get you unpacked then, and I'll take the one over here"—I point behind me—"so that you can be in the room next to your dad."

"*Yay!*" He rushes off to the blue bedroom and I follow.

When we're both unpacked and ready to head out to explore the city, my phone rings in my purse. When I pull it out, I see that it's Hannah making a video call.

This isn't the first time I've seen Hannah on video since Brady and I picked up where we left off, and every time I feel more uncomfortable than the last. I know there's not anything between them, but it still makes me uncomfortable, as though I'm hiding something from Theo's mom.

I hit the green button on my screen and accept the call. "Hi, Hannah."

"Hey, Violet. How are you today?"

"Great. How are things going over there?"

The bags under her eyes are darkening. "Same as always. Not enough people or resources to help, but we're doing our best. Is Theo around? I don't have that much time."

"Of course, here he is." When I look down at Theo, his hand is already outstretched, eager to talk to his mom.

"Hi, Mommy." Theo takes the phone and sits on a nearby chair.

"Hey, buddy. How are you?"

"Awesome. Me and Violet are just going out to see what's around here, then later we're going to swim in the hotel pool."

"Hotel?"

It's clear by the way she says it that this is the first she's heard of our trip. Brady said he would mention it to her, but I'm getting the impression that he didn't.

"Yeah, we're here to see Daddy's game."

I walk over and lean in so I appear on-screen. "We're in Los Angeles to watch the preseason away game, Hannah. I thought Brady was going to mention it to you."

She frowns for a beat. "We got cut off the last time I called him. Maybe he didn't get the chance."

"That's probably it." I put on my best "it's no big deal" voice.

"I'll bet you're going to have so much fun." I can hear in her voice that she wishes she were here. Whether that's because she misses her son or she wishes this was something the three of them did together, I can't tell.

"It's going to be the best!" Sweet little Theo has no idea he's rubbing salt in his mom's wounds.

I lean back into the frame. "I'll text you some pictures of our weekend so you can see what he's up to."

"That'd be great, thank you." She looks over her shoulder, then turns back to the screen. "Okay, I have to go. But I'll give you a call tomorrow when I get a chance."

"Okay, Mommy. I love you." Tears form in his eyes.

Theo's been increasingly teary every time Hannah calls. I think at first maybe Theo didn't realize how long three months was, and now that more time has passed, he's having a harder time with it.

"I love you too. Miss you."

Then she hangs up and Theo holds the phone out to me. His bottom lip is quivering, and my chest squeezes.

I ruffle his hair. "How about we go see if we can find some ice cream before we go for a swim? I think I saw a really cool ice cream shop on the way here."

Slowly his frown turns into a small smile. "Okay."

We head out together and I do my best to distract him

with fun all day long, but nothing can take the place of his mom.

———

Later that afternoon, Theo and I are splashing around in the pool. He's a decent swimmer, though we stay in the shallow end. He's dared me to see if I can swim from the shallow end to the deep end underwater.

"You don't think I can do it?" I tickle his sides and he laughs.

"No way. That's far."

It is pretty far, but I think I have a shot. "Okay, count me down and let's see if I can make it there."

He does, and when he hits one, I drop underwater and push off the wall, kicking my legs and using my arms to move as fast as possible. My eyes are open, and after a bit, I see the wall of the deep end approach. Almost there. Just a few more kicks.

When I touch the wall with my hand, I come up out of the water and gulp some air.

"Yay!" Theo cheers from the other end of the pool. "Do it again."

Holding on to the side, I turn to face him. "Again?" I call, exhausted.

He nods a bunch of times.

"Okay, count me down."

"Three, two, one!"

I slip underwater again and use the wall as leverage to get as far out as I can. It's harder than the last time and I'm not sure if I'm going to make it, but I do. When my hand touches the wall, I pop up out of the water with a cheer, then catch my breath.

The first thing I notice is a set of feet directly in front of me. When I look up, I have to shield my eyes against the sun. It's Brady.

"Thought I'd join you guys."

"Daddy!"

While Theo rushes over to the stairs to greet his dad, Brady gives me the once-over, pausing briefly on my sky-blue bikini top. I do the same to him, taking in his ripped physique in his swim trunks.

Before I say anything and before Theo has even made it to his dad, a woman wearing a black bikini comes up from behind him. "Brady Banks?"

He turns at his name.

"Oh my god, I knew it was you! I told my friend I was right."

Before he can do or say anything, she wraps her swimsuit-clad body around him and hugs him. Theo comes to an abrupt halt, water trickling off his body to the concrete.

To his credit, Brady doesn't return her hug, but it does nothing to soothe the sour feeling in my stomach at the vision of this scantily clad woman all over the man I'm sleeping with. Brady pulls away and sort of sets her back by her shoulders.

"I love you so much! You're the best player in the league."

He gives her a small smile and lets his arms drop from her shoulders. "Thanks, I appreciate that."

"We're going to the game tomorrow." She gestures to a lounger where a woman, who I assume is the other half of the "we," gives a small wave.

"Wonderful. I appreciate the support." He nods and glances at Theo. "I'm just going to have a swim with my son, but it was great to meet you."

The woman gives Theo a cursory glance, then looks at Brady with hearts in her eyes. "Maybe once your little guy is in bed, we can meet up or something? I can give you my room number, or you can tell me yours…" She shifts her hip out in a way I imagine is supposed to be alluring, but it comes off more as desperation in my opinion.

Brady's countenance shifts in a split second. Gone is the patient smile and relaxed posture, and in its place is a face void of emotion and a rigid posture. "It was good to meet you." Then he turns his back to her, picks up Theo, and walks over to the pool stairs.

The urge to pump my fist and cheer is strong, but I resist.

The woman frowns and walks back to her friend in a sulk.

"That was... interesting," I say when Brady walks over to me in the water.

Brady says nothing, but his lips form a thin line.

"Daddy, want to play Marco Polo with me and Violet?"

He looks at his son, who's still in his arms, and he's back to being the Brady I know. "As long as I'm not it."

I cluck my tongue at him. "Those are the rules, I'm afraid."

Brady chuckles. "All right. I'll give you a five-second head start."

Theo yelps and rushes toward the far side of the shallow end. Brady winks at me before closing his eyes and starting his countdown.

The wink gives me flutters in my belly, but I run away from that feeling the same way I'm running away from Brady right now.

thirty-one

. . .

Brady

After the pool, the three of us come up to the room to shower, order room service for dinner, and watch a movie. Theo falls asleep halfway through. Once the credits are rolling, I carry him into his room, gently lay him down, and pull the covers over him.

Violet's lounging on the couch when I come back out to the living area.

"I think all that time in the water really tired him out. Maybe I should get a pool at home." I laugh.

She chuckles as I sit on the opposite side of the couch, then I pull her feet onto my lap to massage them. A moan of appreciation leaves her lips as I dig my thumb into the ball of her foot.

"If football doesn't carry you far, you can give foot massages," she says, resting her head on the armrest of the couch and closing her eyes.

"It's entirely self-serving. I've been thinking of getting my hands on you since I saw you in that bikini earlier."

She opens her eyes and arches an eyebrow. "Is that right?"

I nod slowly. "I had to think about my parents having sex so I wouldn't get a hard-on."

Violet laughs hard, her whole body shaking. "I feel like maybe I'm supposed to apologize."

"Not necessary. It was worth the mental torment to keep myself in check." I set her foot down on my lap and pick up the other one to massage.

"There were lots of bikinis around the pool today. Did you have to think about your parents' sex life the whole time we were down there?"

I tilt my head with a confused expression. "Weird. I didn't even notice any other bikinis."

She rolls her eyes. "Yeah, right. I'm sure you noticed the one pressed up against you when you arrived."

Irritation flares my nostrils at the mention of the woman who tried to pick me up in front of Theo. "Her attention wasn't welcome."

Violet huffs. "She sure made it known that your attention was very welcome to her."

I can't help the shit-eating grin that's spreading across my face. "You're jealous?"

"Please, I'm *not* jealous."

"You so are. Her half-naked body was pressed against what's yours, and she invited me to her room."

Her mouth forms a thin line.

I don't know why I love the idea of Violet being jealous, but I do. I think back to that night she came home tipsy, and I thought maybe she'd brought another man home with her, and suddenly it doesn't feel that funny.

"I have no respect for a woman who propositions me in front of my kid. It shows me that she'd have no respect for my son and that would never work for me. But regardless, there's only one woman I had my eye on at the pool and I'm lucky enough to be giving her a foot rub right now."

That appeases her, and a small smile forms on her lips. "Does that happen often?" Her voice is light and breezy, but something about her body language tells me the air of nonchalance she's putting on isn't authentic.

I don't want to make her more uncomfortable, but there's zero point in trying to soften the truth because she'll figure it out for herself if she continues to come to away games.

"It happens pretty frequently, yeah. But I can tell you with one-hundred-percent honesty that I've never entertained anything with a fan who's approached me. That kind of situation feels rife for conflict to me." I set her foot on my lap.

"What do you mean?"

"I don't know." I shrug. "I was never looking for anything serious and the idea of going home with someone who sought me out because of who I was... it just feels like that kind of woman wouldn't be okay with me bouncing after and never speaking to her again—even if I was honest from the start. I've never had a problem with someone knowing who I am, but the women who approach me as fans... just feel different for me."

She pulls her feet from my lap and nods.

"Sorry, it's kind of weird to have this conversation with you when we're... you know, but I wanted to be honest."

"Honesty's good. Really, I appreciate it."

I'm sure that's probably true, given the situation with her ex-fiancé. I scoot closer to her and rest my hand on her thigh.

"We never did talk about that... whether we were going to be seeing other people while the two of us..." She bites her bottom lip.

I stiffen. Is she trying to tell me that she wants to see other guys while we're messing around?

"Is that something you want?" My eyes narrow and I ignore the sting in my chest.

She must notice because she chuckles. "Now who's jealous?" Then she shakes her head. "No, I don't want that, but I also don't want to assume you're not going to hook up with anyone else if we haven't had the conversation."

I exhale with relief. "Good, because like I said, I only have eyes for one woman right now."

Her smile makes her eyes sparkle. "Great, let's keep it that way."

I bring my lips to hers, coasting my tongue over her lips until she opens for me. When she does, I moan at the taste of her and deepen our kiss.

After a minute, she pulls back and abruptly stands, holding out her hand. "Come with me."

The look in her dark eyes is sinful, so I don't bother asking why. I stand, take her hand, and let her lead me into her bedroom. It's similar to the room I'm staying in, except this one is decorated in tones of champagne and ivory. Violet walks us over to the king-size bed and motions for me to have a seat.

"I'll be back in a minute." She turns.

I watch her ass as she makes her way to the connected bathroom. I sit there with bated breath, waiting for her to reappear. It doesn't take long before she does.

She comes out of the bathroom attached to her bedroom wearing only a black lace thong. My cock instantly hardens at the sight of her tits swaying as she makes her way over to where I sit on the edge of the bed. Her nipples pucker under my attention and I lick my lips, desperate to feel the tightened buds between my teeth. Violet's hair is down in waves, and the look in her eyes is one of determination.

"You look so fucking sexy." My voice is rough like sandpaper, and I rest my hands on her hips when she comes to stand between my legs.

"I thought you might like it." When she pushes both hands through my hair, my eyes drift closed.

When I open them, she's staring at me with possession. Though that might normally spook me, I bask in the satisfaction that she apparently feels as territorial toward me as I do her. My right hand drifts to the space between her thighs to find her panties soaked, but she steps back.

I give her a confused look, and she drops to her knees. "Take your clothes off, Brady."

I'm not an idiot, so I don't waste any time reaching back and pulling my T-shirt over my head, then standing and yanking off my pants and boxer briefs. Then I sit on the edge of the bed again and wait for the sexiest woman I've ever known to do her worst, or her best, as it were.

She draws closer until she's kneeling between my spread legs. I wish I could take a picture—her between my legs, topless, with my hard dick pointing straight up, level with her mouth, her hooded eyes gazing down at it as though she wants to swallow it whole. I'd keep it as a screensaver so I could see it all the time.

Violet meets my gaze as she leans in, opens her mouth slowly, and sucks on the end of my cock.

"Fuuuuck…" I push one hand into her hair and lean back on the other one to enjoy the view.

Her tongue circles the head and she sucks again before letting it fall from her lips. Then she licks me from base to crown, making eye contact the entire time.

Holy fuck. This woman can go from loving caregiver to dirty lover in zero seconds flat and I think this might be one of my favorite things about her. She owns both sides of her personality and I love them both.

Once she's thoroughly soaked most of my hard length with her saliva, she draws me into her mouth and sucks me in as far as she can take me, then pushes even farther so that I push past the back of her throat. I moan as she sucks her cheeks in, making her way back up to the tip.

"Jesus, Violet."

She hums as she brings me back into her mouth, and the vibration of the sound travels down into my balls. Violet picks up the pace a bit and I grip the bedsheet. When she brings one hand to my base and uses it to jerk me while her mouth retreats, I have to work hard not to come. It's not that I don't want to, but I want this sensation to last forever.

I'm a goner when her other hand cups my balls.

My hand tightens in her hair. "Fuck, I'm gonna come."

Violet doesn't pull away. As much as I like the idea of painting her perfect tits with my cum, I hold her head to me while I spill my seed at the back of her throat on a groan, panting at the image before me. She swallows it all, and when I let up, she pulls back and sits on her feet, staring at me with a cheeky smile as though she got exactly what she wanted.

This woman makes me want to worship her with my body and I plan to do just that for the rest of the night.

thirty-two

. . .

Violet

Maybe it was just jealousy, or maybe it was me wanting to make Brady want me so badly he never even looks at another woman again. I have no idea, but I was determined to rock his world with that blow job, and I'd say I was successful.

Afterward, he gave me not one, not two, but three orgasms with his fingers and his mouth. After that, he fucked me doggy style and made me come again.

The man is insatiable. And I'm not complaining.

Now we are lying in bed, cuddled into each other and catching our breath.

"Is this much sex going to be bad for your game this weekend?"

I feel his chest rattle with laughter. "Why would it be bad for my game?"

"I don't know. Don't you athletes have some type of superstitions about stuff like that?"

He strokes his hand over my hip. "Some do, but I don't really subscribe to that kind of thing. And if I did, I can assure you that it wouldn't be to refrain from sex. Hell, if I kill it in the game, I might ask you to blow me before every game."

Now I'm the one laughing. "Oh, if I must, for the good of the team. I volunteer as tribute."

He squeezes my hip with his hand.

"Will your parents be at the game?" I ask.

"Yeah, they're flying in on their plane in the morning. They'll probably be sitting in a box if you and Theo want to join them rather than use the seats I got you."

I shake my head against his hard chest. "That's okay. I think Theo would prefer to be in the middle of all the action."

"Yeah, probably."

We're quiet for a moment, and I assume we're each in our own head.

"It seems like you have a really good relationship with your parents." I'm happy for Brady—and Theo, by extension —but it makes me envious since my relationship with my parents isn't as easy.

"Yeah. It might be a little unconventional. I mean, you've met my mom. And like I told you, growing up in a household where I could just be myself and there was no judgment was a blessing, I think. Though my dad wasn't always like that."

"Oh no?" I shift so I'm propped up on my arm and can look him in the eye.

He shakes his head. "No, that's all my mom's influence over the years. And believe me, she can be a bit much, as I'm sure you can imagine."

I laugh.

"When I was eighteen, she asked me if I'd tried anal yet. Whenever I had a girlfriend over growing up, she'd tell her to let her know if I was a selfish lover because she'd straighten me out."

My hand flies up to cover my mouth. "Oh my god."

"Right? The night I lost my virginity, she knew. I don't know how, but I wasn't in the door more than two minutes before she confronted me with it." He shakes his head as if remembering. "But when I'd fuck up, they never held it against me. They made me take responsibility for it, but I never felt judged."

"I think that's a great way to be for your kids—a soft spot to land."

He nods. "You've kind of alluded to the fact that you might not have the best relationship with your parents… any particular reason?"

I sigh. "My relationship with my parents is complicated. It became even more so when I dropped out of law school to be a full-time nanny."

His eyes widen with surprise. "You were in law school?"

"Yeah, did the first two years. They were so disappointed in me when I left. I swear you'd think I had confessed to being a serial killer. It was like they could think of no worse fate for me than to not end up as a doctor or a lawyer. Then when I called off my engagement, things just got worse. They loved my ex and thought I was a fool for not trying to fix it."

Brady's forehead wrinkles. "Did they know he cheated on you?"

"Yup. But he was a catch. He was five years older than me and already working at a large law firm. My mom thought that I should at least try to make it work, that maybe it was a one-time lapse in judgment for him, but I knew better. He didn't even seem to care that much when I confronted him. It was almost like he was relieved to have been caught so he didn't have to put on the charade of being the doting fiancé anymore."

Brady's hand squeezes my hip. "You're better off without him. He didn't deserve you."

I chuckle and sit up, pulling the sheet up under my armpits. "You don't even know him."

"I know that if he squandered you, he doesn't deserve you. End of story." The fierce glint in his eyes and the steel in his voice make me feel valued and safe.

I place a slow, languid kiss on his lips before rolling back onto my side. "Thank you."

He gives me a sad sort of smile. "So why did you decide to become a nanny?"

I shake my head. "That's the ironic part—a lot of the reason I decided to become a nanny was because of my parents. They spent all their money getting here from South Korea, so they had to work so hard when I was growing up that they were hardly ever around. They were always working at the restaurant. I spent a good part of my child-hood working there too, from an early age. It wasn't that I didn't feel loved—I know they love me—but in some ways, it felt conditional. As long as I had the right grades, went to the right school, got a certain job, they were happy. If not, I just disappointed them."

Brady strokes a piece of my hair behind my ear. "It sounds like the exact opposite of how I grew up."

I nod. "It does. Don't get me wrong, I never begrudged them for working so hard to give my brother and me every-thing we had, but they were always so absent and when they were around, they were so critical of everything. I've never felt good enough where they're concerned."

"You know that's not true though, right?"

A sigh escapes me. "Intellectually, of course I do. But here." I tap my chest over my heart. "Here is a little harder to convince." He frowns, and I'm afraid a look of pity is going to slide onto his face, so I quickly continue. "Anyway, I took a part-time job in college as a nanny, and that's when I realized that I enjoyed being the person to show children love and acceptance—even if they aren't my own."

Other memories from that experience try to push to the forefront, but I slide the lead wall in place. Brady must see something in my face though, because he studies me for a moment and the corners of his lips tip down.

"Anyway, when that job came to an end, I realized how much I would miss being a part of that little boy's life and I asked myself why I was in law school when I really didn't enjoy it. It became clear that I was there to please my parents and because I thought I *should* be there, so I quit. My parents were devastated, and it caused a real strain on our relationship."

"That's tough. I'm sorry."

I shrug. "I know they love me, and I know they only want the best for me. It's just that they seem to think they're the only ones who know what that is. Especially my mom."

His head tilts. "Have you tried telling them how you feel?"

I frown. "Honestly, I can't imagine that conversation. It wouldn't be well received."

"Well, I for one, am glad that you decided to become a nanny, otherwise I'd probably still be trying to hunt you down in random nightclubs."

I chuckle, and without warning, he rolls himself over me so that I'm pinned underneath him. A yelp leaves me, but it turns into a moan as he drags his tongue from my collarbone up to my ear.

"I think you'd manage without me," I say dryly because if this trip has made anything clear to me, it's that Brady certainly has his pick of available women. It's not like I didn't know that before, but seeing it so blatantly thrown in front of me is another thing entirely.

"Bullshit." He pulls back and looks down at me. "It wouldn't be the same if it wasn't you."

Something passes between us, some emotion I don't want to name or dwell on, so I wiggle underneath him and say in a cheeky voice, "Prove it."

A grin transforms his face, and he arches a brow. "Is that a challenge?"

"Most definitely."

Brady rises to the challenge, dragging his tongue down my body under the sheets until his face rests between my thighs, where he does, in fact, prove it. Twice.

thirty-three

· · ·

Violet

"Can I go now?"

I look at Theo, who's practically salivating to run out onto the field.

We're at the training facility again. Brady asked if we wanted to stop by today during their practice, and Theo will take any opportunity to see his dad in action. So will I apparently.

The coach just blew the whistle and told them to take a break, and immediately Brady's attention comes to the sidelines where I'm standing with Theo and Shayna. He takes off his helmet and gives me a small nod.

I tap Theo on the back. "Go ahead, buddy."

He races out to his dad without a backward glance. Brady leans down and scoops him up.

"I think my ovaries just sighed," Shayna says.

I chuckle. "Right? Their relationship is so sweet." I watch them with a smile, and in my peripheral vision, I see Shayna turn to look at me.

"Mind if I ask how things are going with that situation?"

I turn to look at her. Every time I've seen her since our night out, either Brady or one of the other players has been around. We've texted a bit, but I haven't wanted to put anything in writing, so I've been waiting until I had the opportunity to be alone with her. I've filled Amara in on what's going on, but I'd love to get the perspective of someone who's familiar with the team and has her own relationship with a professional football player—though that's not what this is with Brady. Besides, there's a good chance Brady has told Lee, and he's told his fiancée anyway.

After a quick glance to make sure no one is around, I lean closer to her. "We've been messing around ever since the night I was out with you guys."

Shayna's eyes widen and she grins, clapping in a giddy schoolgirl motion.

I take her hands and pull them down before Brady happens to look over and notices. "You really didn't know?"

She shakes her head. "Lee and I agreed not to discuss anything either you or Brady told us after we went out that night and I declared that we were friends."

"Really?" I can't help my smile.

"Of course. Girl code." She holds up her hand like the Boy Scouts do.

I laugh.

"So does this mean you two are dating now or what?" She sounds so hopeful that I almost hate to crush her enthusiasm.

"Or what." She frowns, and I say, "We agreed to keep it just between us and make it simple—we're messing around and nothing more."

"But don't you want—"

I hold up my hand to stop her. "I don't want anything serious. I knew when I broke up with my fiancé last year that I wouldn't be ready for another relationship for a long time. Plus, who knows what Theo's mom would think about it? Not to mention the press if they ever got a hold of it. Plus, neither of us wants to confuse Theo. Brady's protective of him, which I respect, and I don't want to make Theo think I could be a permanent part of his life unless I'm confident that might happen. The truth is, I don't think Brady is really looking for anything serious either. We're just enjoying each other's… company."

Shayna opens her mouth, but she presses her lips together and nods instead.

We're quiet for a minute and look at the field where Brady is tossing Theo the ball. He manages to catch it this time and immediately looks at me.

"Violet, did you see that? I caught it!"

"I saw! Awesome job!" I give him two thumbs up.

He smiles and gives it a half-decent throw to his dad. My attention turns to Brady, who's looking at me, and he catches the ball without even turning his head to look at it.

"Can I just say one thing?" Shayna asks. I manage to turn my attention away from Brady and look at her. "A man who doesn't want anything serious does *not* look at a woman like he's looking at you."

She walks down the sidelines without another word, and I turn to look back at the field. Brady is still watching me until Theo calls for his attention.

When he looks away, my entire body shivers.

———

I park the car, remove the keys, and flop back in my seat, looking at the restaurant sign that's so familiar to me. It's a little faded and sun bleached now, but it brings the familiar sense of nostalgia and hurt it always does.

"Can I have the same thing as last time?" Theo asks from the back seat.

"You don't want to try anything different this time?" I ask, opening the door.

I exit the car and open the back door to help him out.

He shakes his head. "No, I liked that."

"All right. Bulgogi and rice it is then."

He smiles and slides his little hand in mine as we walk to the sidewalk that runs in front of the plaza. Low-level anxiety hums through my veins as we enter the restaurant. The wood tables and flooring are dated, but my parents repainted and reupholstered the chairs a few years ago. My parents say it's the food, not the atmosphere that people come for.

It's lunchtime, so it's fairly busy, but it's as if my mom has radar on me because the moment we walk in, she notices us from the far side of the restaurant. I give her a small wave and smile, waiting for her to have time to greet us.

"Hi, Mom. You remember Theo." I place my hand on his back.

She looks down at him and gives him a nod. "Nice to see you."

"Hi." Theo smiles and waves.

"Are you staying for lunch?" she asks me.

"Figured I'd stop in for a visit since we were around the corner at the training facility."

Her lips press into a thin line and she kind of huffs. Anyone else would be impressed by a professional football player, but not my mother. "You can sit at the table by the register."

We dodge trays of raw meat and banchan dishes to be served and grilled at each table. We take our seats at the small table, but she's not going to sacrifice space for me in case a paying customer comes in. Nor would I want her to. She goes to the next table and takes their order.

When she's done, she turns her attention back to us. "Drinks?"

"Waters. I can get them."

She nods and turns around but turns back. "Make sure you go to the back to say hello to you father."

She tells me this every time as if I wouldn't do it. Usually I'd say something snippy, but since Theo is here and I'm trying to set a good example, I just give her a serene smile. "I will."

With a nod, she turns around and heads to the back to probably tell my dad that his disappointment of a daughter is here to visit.

To keep Theo occupied, I fetch the activity book I always carry around in case we find ourselves somewhere he's going to get bored. I recently showed him how to do word searches. It helps to occupy his time and help him recognize letters and words since I tell him what each word is before he searches for it.

My mom returns with our waters and takes our orders before disappearing into the back. Per usual, she returns shortly after and pulls up a chair. She usually tries to visit while our meal is being prepared. Today she's lucky to have help.

"How was your visit to Los Angeles?" she asks.

"It was fun. I've never been to a professional football game before, so it was an interesting experience. Even though it was only a preseason game, I can't believe how into it the fans get."

She responds in Korean, "I can't believe that man would pay to fly you and his son out there. Waste of money if you ask me."

I speak Korean as well. "Father and son enjoy spending time together. There's nothing wrong with that."

She shrugs in an "if you say so" gesture.

Theo looks up from his activity book. "What are you guys saying?"

"I was just telling my mom about our trip to watch your dad's game."

He looks at my mom. "It was so much fun! That was the first time I got to see him play far away."

My mom gives him a halfhearted smile then points at his book as though he should get back to work. Sometimes it feels as though she's uncomfortable interacting with children, like maybe she doesn't know how.

Theo, being a good-natured boy whose attention is easily diverted, does just that.

"When are you going to give up this silly job and go back to school?" my mom asks, as she does every time I see her.

I glance at Theo, who's concentrating on his word search and doesn't seem to have heard her now that she's speaking English. Probably so the other Korean families in the restaurant don't hear. Just in case, I take out my earbuds and his tablet.

"How about some *Hey, Arnold*?"

Theo looks as if I just said it's Christmas morning. I never usually allow him to watch television at restaurants, but my mom and I are about to get into it. He shouldn't have to hear any of that.

Once he's settled, I respond to her. "I don't know how many times I can tell you that's not going to happen before you'll believe me. I don't want to be a lawyer. I never really did."

"Instead, you drive around a bunch of rich people's kids for them. You could be the rich person if you went back to school."

My hands form into fists on the table. "I understand that money is important, but it's not the only route to happiness. I want to love what I do and enjoy my work every day. Besides, I make a good living as a nanny. In another six months or so, I should have enough for my down payment to look for my own place."

"A lawyer is respected. A doctor is respected. This nanny job isn't for a well-educated woman."

It takes me half a minute of deep breaths to calm myself enough to respond. "Maybe not to you, but I'd like to think the families I help respect me."

Theo's little voice pipes up. "Violet's the best nanny. I have so much fun with her."

So much for the earbuds. Tears form in my eyes. This sweet little boy is trying to stick up for me.

I can't help but squeeze his hand. That's when I notice he has *Hey, Arnold* on pause and he was eavesdropping on our conversation. He gives me a big smile. It's so filled with innocence, like he believes his words and his smile can fix years of heartache, that I could weep.

"Thank you, Theo."

He nods and looks back down at his tablet.

Not wanting to continue this conversation in front of him, I change the subject. "I spoke with Eric last week. Heard he's decided to put his proposal off until New Year's Eve."

As expected, my mom's face lights up. "Isn't that such a great idea?"

Yeah, real original. "Such a great idea." I strain to smile. "Have you seen the ring?"

She nods. "He sent me a picture. It's so big. But that's what you get on a doctor's salary, I suppose."

I literally have to bite my bottom lip not to comment.

We chat for a couple more minutes about how the restaurant is doing, then she pushes back from the table and says she's going to check on our meals.

Once she's away from the table, Theo looks at me. "Why do we come here? She makes you sad. But don't worry, I'm gonna make you happy like you help me when I'm sad about my mom."

This time, a tear does sneak loose, and it is one of sadness, but not for my mother. It's because I'm going to miss this little guy as much as his father when it's time for me to say goodbye.

thirty-four

. . .

Brady

"All right, buddy. That's it for tonight." I close the book and kiss the top of his head.

"Just one more?" he whines.

"It's time for bed." I use my dad voice so he knows not to bother arguing.

He relents, scooting down from where he was sitting against the headboard so he's lying down with his head on his pillow. "Daddy, how much longer is Violet going to be here?"

Where is this question coming from? Does he want her to leave?

My forehead wrinkles. "She's with us for a little less than two more months, buddy."

"Then what?" he asks.

"Mommy comes home, and Violet goes to help another family." I hate the way my stomach squeezes painfully at the thought of her absence from our lives.

"Oh." I can't tell if he's happy or sad about that.

"Why do you ask?" I scoot down to lie beside him with my head propped on my hand.

"We saw her mom at the restaurant today and they were talking about it. Her mom makes her sad." He frowns.

I see how much that upsets him. It upsets me too, truth be told, knowing what she's told me about her relationship with her parents.

"Sometimes other people think they know what's best for someone and they get upset if that person doesn't do it. But I wouldn't worry about it. Violet will be fine." I taste the lie on my tongue because it's clear to me the effect her parents' feelings about her life have on her, but I'm not going to get into that with my almost six-year-old son. Which is the perfect segue into happier thoughts for my little man. "Are you excited for your birthday party next week?"

He nods excitedly. "It's gonna be so fun."

"Can't wait." I give him a kiss. "Hard to believe you're going to be six already." Theo smiles proudly as though six is a big accomplishment, and I ruffle his hair. "All right, you get a good sleep. I'll see you tomorrow. Love you."

"Love you too, Daddy."

I get up off the bed and flick off his lamp, then quietly leave the room, closing the door behind me.

I head to my room to have a shower and my dick is hard the entire time I'm under the water, but I don't allow myself to rub one out. I'm saving myself for Violet. Sure, I could go find her and take her right now, but we usually wait a bit until after Theo is in bed so we're sure he's asleep. Plus, I don't want to seem like I'm smothering her and can't get enough. Even though that's the truth.

After I've dried off and changed into lounge pants and a T-shirt, I leave my room to head downstairs. When I pass her room, her door is open and I can't help but notice a box sitting in the middle of her bed. I wouldn't invade her privacy, but it's a familiar-looking box, so I go in and pick it up off the bed.

Yep. It's a hot-pink vibrator in the shape of a crooked *L*.

Shaking my head, I take the box downstairs. I find Violet in the family room, watching TV, and I stand in front of her, blocking the view of the TV.

"Hey... what's going on?" She obviously knows something's up.

"Found this on your bed." I motion with the box, but I'm holding it so she can only see the back of the box, not what's inside.

"What is it?"

I turn the box around and watch as understanding dawns. Her mouth falls open, her eyes widening. "I swear that isn't mine, Brady. I have no idea how it got there."

I do. "You mentioned that my parents swung by to see Theo today?"

She nods, eyes still wide.

"This is my mom's handiwork." I hold up the box and point at the logo. "This is her company."

Her eyes practically bug out of her head. "Your mom gave me a vibrator?"

I shrug. "I warned you. She has zero boundaries. Knowing her, this is some new model they're working on and she's going to want to pick your brain about it after you use it."

Her eyes widen even more, which I wouldn't have thought possible, so I laugh.

"I'll talk to her about not leaving this stuff in your room."

"Well, I mean, as long as Theo doesn't see it." She bites her lip.

I set the box on the coffee table and sit beside her. "Am I finding the kinky side of Violet?"

She shrugs. "You do travel a lot."

"Ohhh... I'll have my mom's company make one of my own for you."

She laughs, and I tug her toward me.

"Nothing is as good as the real thing." Her hand falls between my legs and she cups my already hard dick.

Even though I want to fuck her right now, I don't want her to think that's all our relationship is. "How was your day?"

"It was good. Nothing special."

I'm disappointed that she didn't open up with me about her visit with her mom, which is stupid. We're not supposed to be anything more than fuck buddies, I suppose.

"Theo's really excited about his birthday party next week."

She smiles and sits up straighter. "It's so hard keeping all the details to myself. I want to tell him all about it so I can see his reaction."

I chuckle. "You'll get to see it at the party."

"I know. I'm just not a very patient person." She smiles.

I can't help but kiss her. What can I say? It's a fucking turn-on when a woman seems to care as much for your child as you do.

When I deepen the kiss, she draws back. "Theo's in bed?"

"Yep." I lean in to kiss her again, but she places her finger over my lips.

"We should wait a bit to make sure he's not going to get out of bed. I'm going to go have a bath, then I'll meet you in your room."

"You just had your hand on my dick," I say.

She laughs. "Because I didn't want him jealous that I wanted the vibrator." She stands. "So, I'll meet you in your room?"

I don't know why she phrases it as a question. We've been together practically every night since our "arrangement" came to pass. And usually in my bedroom since hers shares a wall with Theo's room.

"I'll be not so patiently waiting." I sneak a chaste kiss.

"Behave." She gets up off the couch with a grin and leaves the room.

I sit there and try to watch TV for about fifteen minutes, but my cock is hard because my mind keeps wandering to the image of a naked Violet relaxing in a warm bath. Plus, my gaze keeps drifting to the box on the coffee table.

"Fuck it." I grab the box, reading the details on the back.

Waterproof.

Perfect. Just what I was hoping for.

I rip open the box like Theo might on Christmas morning and breathe a sigh of relief that it takes a charge or batteries. No time for charging. And because my mother knows human nature and is a smart businesswoman, a pair of batteries is included. I insert them into the vibrator and press a button to make sure it works, smiling when it buzzes in my hand.

Taking the stairs two at a time, I race upstairs and tiptoe past Theo's room over to Violet's. The door is closed but not locked. I crack it open to find the room empty, but the bathroom door closed. I head into the room, closing the door, then knock softly at the en suite door.

"Hello? Brady?" Her voice sounds hesitant.

I open the door and find her in the large tub, surrounded by bubbles. Her hair is pulled up into a messy bun to keep it out of the water.

"Is everything okay?" she asks.

"Yup." I close the door. "I just thought of a way to help you better relax in here." I bring the vibrator out from around my back.

She doesn't say anything, but her tongue darts out and licks her bottom lip before she bites it. I take that as my invitation and walk over to the tub. Violet doesn't miss the erection tenting my cotton pants.

There's a look of almost disappointment on her face when I don't strip down to join her in the tub, but not only do I want this to be about her, but I have my phone in my pants to alert me if Theo leaves his room. If he finds me in here with her, it'll be pretty hard to come up with an excuse he'll believe.

When I kiss her, she sighs into my mouth. I slip my hand

under the water, then press the button that makes the long end vibrate, hitting it a few times until I find the rhythm I want. Then I drag it between her legs, and they fall open for me.

Ending our kiss, I pull away and watch her eyelids grow heavy as I concentrate the tip on her clit. She undulates, making the water splash and ripple, and she sucks in a breath, holding my gaze. When I take the vibrator away, she's panting, tiny beads of perspiration forming at her hairline. Whether it's from the warmth of the water or the intensity of the feeling, I'm not sure.

When I bring it back between her legs, I move it around the rim of her opening, allowing it to just breach her entrance but not pushing it in. She makes a whining sound in the back of her throat every time I take it away.

Only once she's panting and begging me wordlessly with her eyes do I give her the satisfaction of pushing it all the way in. She breaks eye contact, her head flopping back on the back of the tub, eyes closing. I push the button to increase the vibration now that it's inside her and push the second button to turn on the part that rests near her clit and creates a subtle sucking motion with air.

Her hands fly out of the water, splashing me, and she grips the sides of the tub.

"You like that?" I ask.

Her hips roll under the water. I pull the vibrator from her a bit then push it back in as though I'm fucking her with it. She nods, but I want to hear the words.

"Tell me what you want, Violet. Tell me and I'll give it to you."

She straightens her head and looks at me.

God, she's so fucking beautiful like this, on the precipice of coming. Her cheeks are rosy, her breathing is heavy, and her eyes read, "give it to me and you can take every piece of me."

"Say it and it's yours, beautiful."

"Fuck me with it. Make me come."

The words are barely out of her mouth before I hit both buttons, increasing the vibration and the suction, then I fuck her with it just like she wants.

She arches with a groan, causing her tits to pop out of the water. I suck one nipple into my mouth and she moans some more. The bubbles don't taste great, but my cock doesn't care, stiffening even more. When she's just about there, I push it in and swivel it around. She goes rigid, crying out. I cover her mouth with my hand to keep her from waking Theo while she rides out her orgasm, water splashing over the sides of the tub.

I pull the vibrator from her and turn it off, pulling it from the water and setting it on the bathmat as her eyes drift open.

Violet slowly rolls her eyes and turns her head to look at me. "I am so relaxed now."

My head flies back on a laugh.

It's a rare woman who can make you want to come and laugh, all within the same minute.

"I knew it was a good plan." I kiss her.

It's all I can do not to strip and join her in the bathtub for round two, but I need to have some self-control around this woman, so I force myself to leave, counting down the minutes until she's done with her bath and joining me in my bedroom.

thirty-five

. . .

Violet

It's the day of Theo's birthday party and I'm outside, putting the final touches on the decorations before we bring him out here to have a look. He's in his room playing since he can't see the backyard from his bedroom.

There's a jumping castle for the kids and an activity table that, of course, has Lego on it. A rainbow of balloons greets guests at the side entrance of the house into the backyard, and every napkin, tablecloth, and plate has something Lego on it. Brady's instructions were not to go too overboard—he didn't want a lavish party like some celebrities throw their kids— but I think this is a happy medium and I really hope Theo will love it.

Brady ran out to pick up the cake I ordered—which looks like a bunch of different-colored Lego bricks stacked together —and when he returns, we'll bring Theo out to have a look.

With my hands on my hips, I survey the table one last time, making sure everything we need is there.

Candles.

I'll bring them out here now so we're not searching for them when it's time to do the cake.

I head inside and go in the pantry and flick on the light. I know I put the candles in here the day I went to get all the party supplies. After a minute of searching, I find them behind a box of cake mix. I grab them and spin around, yelping when I crash into a hard body. Brady steadies me with both hands on my upper arms.

"You scared me."

"I see that." He chuckles, and I swat him with my free hand but stop when he leans in to kiss me. "I took a peek out back. Everything looks fantastic. He's gonna love it. Thank you."

I smile. "It's my pleasure. It was actually a lot of fun."

Brady tucks a piece of hair behind my ear, then reaches back and closes the pantry door so we're sealed inside— alone. I don't have to ask what he's up to because the pantry is our go-to make-out spot whenever Theo is up. We've basically turned the pantry into our own sex dungeon.

No sooner has Brady wrapped his arms around me and brought his mouth down to mine than we hear Theo calling from the other side.

"Daddy? Daddy, where are you?"

With a sigh and a chuckle, Brady backs away from me and opens the door. "Right here, buddy."

Theo pops into view as I follow Brady out of the pantry. His forehead is wrinkled. "What are you guys doing in there?"

"Your dad was helping me find the candles for your cake." I hold up the candles as though they're evidence that we weren't up to anything else.

Theo's smile grows. "Can I see the backyard now?"

"Anything for you, birthday boy." I walk past him and ruffle his hair. "Follow me."

I lead Theo and Brady out to the back and no sooner is the door open than Theo races outside.

"This is awesome!" His eyes are as wide as I've ever seen

them as he stands in place and circles around, taking it all in. "Wait until my friends get here!"

"I'm so happy you like it." My heart feels as if it's going to beat out of my chest when Theo wraps his arms around my legs, hugging me.

"I love it. Thank you."

I run my hand through his hair. "You're so welcome."

I glance at Brady, and he has the strangest look on his face until he blinks and clears his throat.

"All right, should we go get you changed into your Lego shirt?" Brady asks.

Theo lets me go and runs into the house, leaving the two of us alone. Brady leans forward for a second as though maybe he's going to kiss me, then seems to think better of it, reaching for my shoulder instead and squeezing it before retreating into the house.

I don't know what's going on in his head. He's seemed more intense lately, more desperate for me, and I'm certainly not complaining. But he hasn't brought up anything about wanting to change our arrangement, so maybe it's all in my head.

It's just as well anyway. Surviving the end of my relationship with my ex was bad enough. I honestly don't know if I could pull myself out of that hole if I allowed myself to think that there could really be something between us and it didn't come to pass.

———

The party is in full swing, and Theo is having a blast in the jumping castle with his friends. I've met some members of Brady's extended family as well as some of the other Kingsmen players, most of whom don't seem to be attached since they didn't bring anyone. It's as if every player on the team is a perpetual bachelor.

I'm refilling the chip bowl when Brady's mom comes up to me. "You're doing a great job with Theo, Violet. I have to say, this party shows how much you care about him. Brady told me you put most of it together."

I crumple the empty chip bag in my hands. "Brady did his part."

Lennon waves me off. "Please, we both know the woman carries the weight of these kinds of events. The boys are lucky to have you."

"Theo is a really special kid."

She looks over to where he's trying to convince his friend Kale—who's scared to go into the jumping castle—to join everyone.

"He sure is." She watches him for a beat, then returns her attention to me. "I've been meaning to ask you if you liked my gift."

My cheeks get hot even as I try to feign innocence. "Gift?"

She grins. "Don't be coy. You know what I'm talking about."

I glance around as though anyone else would have any idea we're talking about a sex toy. "It was great."

She scowls. "Great? We need to go back to the drawing board then because great is not good enough. I'm looking for feedback like mind blowing."

It's clear that I'm not going to get away from this conversation until I'm honest. But not too honest. "Well, it was that and then some."

Her smile makes her eyes sparkle. "That's what I want to hear. Did you find the suction too much? We've made it adjustable, and it'll blow in or out so that the user can change it according to their preference. No two pussies are the same, I always say."

My breath stops in my lungs and I glance around. No one other than Brady is paying us any attention. I see, now that he's spotted me talking to his mom, that he's wrapping up his conversation with a player from his team and making his way over here.

"I thought the adjustments were great. I'm sorry, will you excuse me, Lennon? I'm going to go get everything for the cake ready."

She squeezes my forearm. "Sure thing, sweetheart. And please know if you're ever in need of anything my company might supply, all you have to do is call. Think of me as your sex toy fairy, your naughty nymph, your peak purveyor." She laughs.

"Okay, will do. Thanks." I give her a small wave and turn quickly to head toward the house, passing Bryce and Shayna on my travels.

"Saw you talking to Brady's mom. Judging by the look on your face, you got an earful," Bryce says with a laugh.

I stop to stand with them. "You guys, I don't know what to make of her. I've never met someone so sexually free, which is great, but at the same time, holy hell."

The three of us laugh.

"She asked how many times a week I masturbate earlier," Bryce says, bringing her beer to her lips.

"Are you serious?" The expression on Shayna's face is comical. It's a mixture of horror and awe.

"What did you say?" I ask.

Bryce shrugs. "I told her once or twice if I'm getting some good *D* on the side, three or four if not."

"You should have told her your pussy's a man-eater and you can't shove anything up there," Miles says, passing us.

"Screw you, Miles." Bryce rolls her eyes.

"And on that note, I'll see you guys in a bit." I motion toward the house.

"Where are you headed?" Shayna asks.

"I'm going to get the cake. Theo hasn't seen it yet. I can't wait to show him."

Both women smile at me, but it's the way they smile at me that makes me pause.

"What? Why are you both looking at me that way?"

"No reason," Shayna says.

"Just that you look like a woman in love, that's all." Bryce shrugs.

My mouth falls open. "Bite your tongue."

Then I race into the house as if the devil is on my heels.

thirty-six

· · ·

Brady

I make my way over to where my mom is chatting up Violet, but before I get there, Violet takes off toward the house.

My mom must really be on a roll then. Great.

"Having a good time?" I ask her once I reach her.

"The best! It's always great to see my grandson so happy." She gestures behind me and I turn to stand beside her so we can watch as Theo jumps around like a madman inside the jumping castle, laughing the whole time.

"Agreed." I take a pull off my beer.

"Violet really did a great job with the party. I'm impressed."

I look around at all the effort she put in. Yes, she's on my payroll, but I know she didn't do any of this for a paycheck. She did this because she cares about Theo. "Yeah, she worked hard on it."

"Mmmhmm."

I'm content to stand there for a moment and watch all the kids, but I should know better than to assume my mom will stop there.

"So… is the sex good?"

I groan, and my head tilts back so I'm staring at the sky. "How is it possible that I'm not in therapy?"

She laughs.

I straighten and look at her. "What are you even talking about?"

My mom gives me a disappointed look. "Don't try to deny it. I'm not an idiot."

"What does that mean?" I scowl.

"The chemistry between you two is palpable. And no one looks at each other the way you two do if they aren't fucking." She picks up a handful of goldfish crackers and eats them.

"All right, tone it down. We're at a kid's birthday party."

She shrugs. "Tell me I'm wrong."

I debate doing that for half a second, but it will do no good. My mom is insightful and persistent.

"We are. But it's nothing serious, so don't give me that look," I say and point at her when she practically gets heart eyes as though she's going to marry me off. "We've talked about it and neither of us wants it to be anything serious. We're just acting on our attraction to one another and when it's done, it's done."

My mom shakes her head. "She's drinking the same idiot water as you?"

"Excuse me?"

"You don't really think that you don't have feelings for her, do you, Brady?"

I take a pull from my beer. "I told you. It's casual."

She frowns. "There's nothing casual about the way you look at her. Especially when she's with Theo."

I hate the way her words resonate with me. I open my mouth to defend myself but find I can't. Thank God my dad chooses that moment to interrupt us.

My mom turns and looks at him proudly. "Brady and Violet are sleeping together."

I pinch the bridge of my nose. "Mom?"

"I didn't say fucking," she says, dead serious as if I should thank her.

"This has to be the only family that gives updates to each other about their sex lives."

"You finally told her, huh?" He wraps his arm around my mom, but she leans away from him and looks between the two of us.

"Wait. Jasper, you already knew?"

My dad shrugs. "I knew the day she first showed up here."

She swings around to look at me. "You slept with her on her first day?"

My dad's head whips in my direction with an "oh shit" expression. Clearly, he did as I asked and kept the fact that I'd slept with Violet before she was Theo's nanny to himself. And now he's gonna be in the doghouse because of it.

My phone vibrates in my back pocket, and I pull it out to see that it's Hannah. "I'm gonna leave you to explain, Dad. Have fun."

I don't waste any time answering the call in case either of my parents tries to pull me back in to run interference. "Hey, Hannah. How are you?" It's clear right away that she's been crying. "Everything okay?"

"Yeah, I'm just sad I can't be there for Theo's birthday. It's hitting me harder than I expected."

I frown and walk more to the side where she won't have to overhear the party. "I'm sorry. Give me a second, he's in the bouncy castle. Let me get him for you."

It takes me a minute to get Theo's attention among all the jumping kids, but I do, and when I tell him his mom is on the phone, he immediately bounces over to me.

"Let's take the call away from everyone so you can hear, okay?" I say.

He nods and runs closer to the house, not waiting for me.

"Here you go." I hand him the phone.

"Hi, Mommy!"

"Happy birthday, little man!"

"Mommy, you should see my party. Everything is Lego!"

"Oh wow. Well maybe your dad can send me some pictures later."

Theo looks up at me over the phone, and I nod. "He says he will."

"Wonderful. So what have you been doing all day so far?"

They chat for a minute or two while Theo tells her all about the fun he's having at his birthday party, then Hannah says she has to go.

"Do you have to go already, Mommy?" Theo whines.

"I'm sorry, bud, but I do. But listen, I wrapped a present for you before I left. Your dad will make sure he gives it to you when you open them all."

Tears fill his eyes as Theo tilts his head and frowns. "But I want you to be here when I open it."

Hannah sighs. "I wish I could be there. I'm really sad that I'm not."

"Why couldn't you come home for my birthday?" he asks, and the tears are replaced by anger for the first time.

This feels like the right time for me to step in. "Buddy, you know why. Your mom is on the other side of the world with a bunch of people who really need her help."

We talked about this last week when he asked whether Hannah would be here or not for the party.

"But I want Mommy here. I miss her! I need her!" he yells.

"I'm sorry I can't be there, Theo. I really wish I could." Hannah tries to console him from over the phone, but this is a side of Theo I've never seen before.

Who am I kidding? We've been watching this pot boil for a long time. Why didn't we predict it would boil over one day?

"No, you don't or you'd be here!" He tosses the phone into the grass and races into the house.

"Shit," I mumble, bending to pick up the phone from the grass. I hold it up in front of me and Hannah's head is in her hands. She's crying uncontrollably. "Don't cry, Hannah. He didn't mean it."

"I should be there with him. I thought I could handle it, but I can't believe I'm missing his birthday." She wipes the wetness under her eyes.

"He'll have more. He's just been missing you a lot lately, and he was up late last night and up early today because he was excited for his party. He's just tired."

She shakes her head as though none of that means anything. "He hates me."

"He doesn't hate you. Give us a call tomorrow when you can, and I promise he'll be back to his usual happy self when you talk to him."

"All right. Thanks, Brady. Make sure to tell him I love him."

I nod. "Will do. Talk to you tomorrow."

I hit End Call and blow out a breath, pushing a hand through my hair. Shoving my phone in my back pocket, I head inside in search of Theo. A quick search of the main level comes up empty, so I head upstairs, thinking he's probably gone to his room.

I hear Violet before I see her. "Your mom loves you so much, Theo. If she could be here, she would."

Theo's sniffles are like a dagger to the heart.

I come to a stop beside the door and lean in so I can see inside. Violet is lying on the bed facing away from me and she has her arms around Theo, who is rolled into her chest, holding on for dear life. He mumbles something I can't make out.

"You should be so proud of your mom, Theo. Do you

know how selfless and brave she's being, helping all those people who don't have anywhere to live right now?"

He pulls back from her a bit and looks up at her. "Why don't they have anywhere to live?"

"Where they live isn't safe anymore, so they had to go to a different country. Your mom is making sure they're healthy. She's helping little kids like you."

"I know, but it's my birthday."

Violet nods and rubs his back. "I know and it's a huge sacrifice you're making, but she's pretty special if you ask me. And I know she's just as upset as you."

God, this fucking woman is a saint. My chest is about to burst right now watching her console my son.

"I miss her." Theo cries again.

"I know you do, sweetie. Of course you do. She misses you too, but we're halfway through her time being away. You can be brave and do another half, right?" She looks at him, and he nods reluctantly.

"I didn't say bye to my mom when she called." Theo looks as though he might cry again.

"You know what? You're pretty lucky both your parents love you so much and I know they won't hold it against you. They know how much you love them."

He seems to think about it for a minute, then nods. They hug again and Violet squeezes extra tight, making Theo laugh.

"All right, you ready to go back and have some fun at your party? I was just about to bring your cake out when you ran in. Want to see what it looks like?"

He rolls away from her and off the bed. "Yeah!"

I quickly back away from the door and make it to the stairs before they emerge from the bedroom, but they catch me at the top of the stairs.

"Everything okay?" I ask nonchalantly.

Theo doesn't seem to clue in that I was eavesdropping, but Violet gives me a little grin and I know I've been caught.

"Yep. I'm taking Theo down to get a look at his cake."

"C'mon, Daddy." Theo grabs my hand as he passes me.

I head downstairs with him, Violet right behind us. When we reach the landing, I look over my shoulder and mouth "thank you" to her, but it doesn't feel like words are enough to express the feeling burning inside me.

thirty-seven

. . .

Violet

Theo crashes shortly after all the presents are opened, the cake is eaten, and the guests have left. I'd say the party was a success except for the one hiccup after he talked to his mom.

The poor little guy. I saw him run past the kitchen in tears and there was no way I couldn't go after him. I felt as if my heart was bleeding out of my chest seeing him like that.

I know Brady overheard me talking to Theo in his bedroom. While I don't think he would have an issue with anything I said, he's been looking at me strangely all night. I'll look in his direction and find him watching me, studying me almost as if he's trying to figure me out. So when I knock on his bedroom door an hour after Theo went down, as per our usual routine, I'm a little nervous, though I can't explain exactly why.

"Come in."

I open the door and find Brady lying in bed watching the sports channel, shirtless, wearing a pair of lounge pants. If I snapped a picture right now, he'd look as if he was in an ad, he's so effortlessly handsome and sexy.

"Hey," he says and picks up the remote and clicks off the TV.

I close the door and lock it.

"Hey. How do you think today went?" I crawl onto the bed and rest my back on the headboard beside him. For whatever reason, I'm nervous to hear his answer. I just want him and Theo to think I did a good job, I guess.

"I think Theo had a sixth birthday party he'll never forget. Thank you for everything you did to make it happen." His gaze darts around my face as though he's searching for something.

I smile. "I think Theo had fun. Except for that one blip, but he got back into the swing of things quickly."

"Thank you for that." His voice is as soft as worn leather. "He was missing his mom and you stepped in and made him feel better. I can't convey how much that meant to him, how comforted he was by your touch and your words."

My cheeks heat. "I just did what anyone would do."

He shakes his head and shifts so one shoulder is leaning against the headboard and he's facing me. "No, you went above and beyond, just like you have the entire time you've been here." Brady cups my cheek and I lean into his touch. "My son is lucky to have you in his life and so am I."

My chest swells with a sensation I've never felt before. It's almost like a rolling wave of warmth cascades through me.

Brady brings his lips to mine and kisses me slowly, his hand still on my cheek. He's never kissed me this slowly, this languidly, as though we have all the time in the world. As though he's pouring every emotion inside him into our kiss.

After a few minutes, he pulls me onto his lap so that I'm straddling him. I feel his hard length against my core, and we both moan at the friction when I gently rock my hips.

Brady weaves his hands into the hair on either side of my face, gazing up at me with hazel eyes spilling over with what I think is love. "I knew there was something special between us the night we first met. I just didn't know it could be this good."

His words are a balm to my soul, and until he said them, I didn't realize how badly I needed to hear them. I lean in and kiss him, trying to tell him without words how much he means to me.

Brady reaches for the hem of my shirt and slowly lifts it over my head. Only then do we break our kiss. When I'm topless, he wastes no time closing his mouth over my left nipple. He kisses it the way he kisses my mouth, his tongue exploring and prodding, then drags his tongue over to my other breast and does the same. One of his hands slips beneath the elastic waistband of my sleep shorts and his fingers slide into my sex.

"Always so wet for me," he mumbles against the hot skin on my chest.

My hips move of their own accord, desperate for more. His fingers skim over my clit and a breathless moan escapes my lips, but Brady catches it with his mouth, swallowing the sound.

He pushes one, then two fingers into me, and my body, unbidden, moves up and down, riding them. The friction from my nipples rubbing against his hard chest tightens the muscles in my core and I squeeze his fingers inside me.

Brady groans and pulls his fingers from me, then flips us so that he's on top, staring down at me in awe, almost as if he can't believe I'm here. He leans back on his heels and slowly drags the cotton shorts down my legs, leaving me naked.

"Your turn." I nod toward his lounge pants tented with his erection.

Wordlessly, he stands at the side of the bed and pulls down his pants, stepping out of them. The man's body is a work of art, and when he lays his weight down on me, I have to stop myself from moaning at just the feel of his heated skin against my own.

Brady kisses me, and this time it's different. It's not our usual fast beat at a nightclub, as if we can't get enough of one another. This kiss is like a slow jazz number that rises and falls as if we never want it to end.

My arms wrap around his neck and my legs fall open for him to nestle his hips between them. Still, the head of his hard length bumps against my sex and makes me desperate to feel him inside me.

His tongue explores my mouth, and my hands play with the hair at the back of his head until I'm strung so tight I'm going to snap. Only then does he pull away from our kiss and prop himself up on his elbows, meeting my eyes as he pushes inside me.

Slowly, so slowly, he enters me, and with every inch of progress, I feel as if I'm being filled with more emotion than I know how to deal with. He doesn't break our eye contact as he moves in and out of me, his pace steady and sure. The feelings I have for this man swell up inside me until I'm near bursting and I have to press my lips together to keep from voicing them.

His fingers trail through my hair while his hard length slides through my slick heat. Then his lips descend, gently kissing my forehead, my cheeks, my nose. He doesn't say anything, but with each press of his lips to my skin, I *feel* what he's not saying—that this is special, that this time is different, that he doesn't want to let me go.

My orgasm hits me like a slow rolling tide, swelling up until it overtakes me entirely and I come with a cry. He swallows the sound when he kisses me and stills, emptying himself inside me right after.

We remain in that position, eyes locked, until he grows soft inside me. He pulls out, and his cum leaks out between my thighs. After one last kiss, he climbs off the bed and goes into his bathroom, returning with a wet cloth that he places between my legs, cleaning me.

After he's done the same for himself in the bathroom, he slides under the covers and motions for me to join him. I slip beneath them and cuddle into his side, wrapping my arm over his stomach.

"Thank you for a wonderful day." He kisses the top of my head.

"You don't have to keep thanking me." My voice is soft. I feel exposed and raw after what we just did.

"I do though." He squeezes me.

We lie there for a few minutes, the two of us caught up in our own heads. My mind spirals into thoughts of what this means. Has anything changed? If it has, do I want that? I want to flee so I can be alone with the thunderstorm of thoughts brewing in my head.

I shift to get off him. "I should probably get back to my room now before I fall asleep. Long day."

Brady frowns. "Stay for just a little longer?"

He's never asked me to stay before. It's an unwritten rule that I have to retreat to my own bed in case Theo finds us. And though I shouldn't, today I can't deny myself the indulgence, so I settle back against the warmth of his chest.

"Okay, a bit."

Panic tries to push out the peace I feel. It's clear that something has shifted, and I have no idea what that might mean for us. I'm afraid to hope it means something good.

thirty-eight

. . .

Brady

A few days have passed since Theo's birthday party, and neither Violet nor I have brought up what happened that night. It's as though we're both trying to pretend that we didn't make love.

In fact, the very next day, she surprised me in the pantry with a blow job. I couldn't help but wonder if it was more about getting us back to a place where our sexual encounters were tinged with lust rather than emotions.

For my part, I've been sitting with my feelings, trying to figure out what they mean. I don't want to say something I don't mean and end up hurting Violet down the road, so I have to be sure before I suggest making this tryst of ours something more serious and permanent.

I honestly have no idea how she'd react if I told her I wanted more from her. I know her ex really fucked with her head, and the chasm that exists between her and her parents affects her more than she lets on too.

There's just so much to consider: Theo, my career and how Violet would handle my absences, the media attention and other women's advances. Then there's how Hannah will react —not that she has a say in who I choose to bring into my life.

But the truth is that neither of us has been in a serious relationship since we split when Theo was little. We haven't had to deal with the other person having a significant other in their lives. There're sure to be some growing pains.

"Fuck," I grumble and push a hand through my hair.

"You said a bad word," Theo says on our walk back from the park. I told Violet I would take him while she cleaned up after lunch.

"Sorry, buddy. My bad."

Today is a rare day off and I want to enjoy it with my son, but my mind has been going nonstop, thinking about all this stuff with Violet. So much for the light and breezy affair we'd planned on having.

If I'm honest with myself, I knew it would never be a casual encounter for me. Something about Violet has pulled me to her since the first night we met.

It's that thought that makes me decide I need to have a conversation with Violet today. I'm certain she's having a lot of the same thoughts, and there's no point in each of us stressing out and wondering what the other is thinking when we can just have a conversation and sort it out.

I'm heading out of town to our final preseason game in Green Bay and I don't want this on my mind while I'm away. I have a job to do, and I need to be able to focus.

Violet and Theo won't be joining me this time because Theo has his orientation for school while I'm gone, and Violet is taking him.

We arrive back home, and as soon as we're through the door, Theo races ahead to go find Violet. I follow. She's in her room, stripping the bedding from her mattress to wash her sheets.

"How was the park?" she asks Theo with a smile.

"Daddy pushed me as high as I could go on the swings!" He's all smiles and oozing energy. It's like the park did nothing to burn off some of the excess.

"Oh wow, we'll have to see if I can get you higher than your dad did the next time we go." She winks.

I chuckle. "Challenge accepted."

Theo whips around to face me. "Daddy, want to do that new Lego set I got for my birthday?" He bounces up and down, waiting for my answer.

It's always amusing to me how fast kids can go from one thing to the next.

"Just give me a few minutes. There's something I need to talk to Violet about."

"Okay, I'm gonna get it all out."

He rushes out of the room, and I hear him hurrying down the stairs.

"Use the railing!"

"I know," he shouts back.

I push my hands in my pockets and turn to face Violet. She's standing by the edge of the bed, frozen with a sheet rumpled in her hands. I recognize that she's clued into what I want to address and she looks as if she could bolt at any moment. I walk over to her, take the sheet, and toss it in the nearby laundry hamper, then I take her hands and lead her to the edge of the bed where we both sit.

"Don't look so scared." I tuck a piece of errant hair that's escaped her ponytail behind her ear.

"I'm not scared."

I tilt my head and raise an eyebrow. "You look like you're either going to throw up or run out of here."

She draws in a deep breath and sighs. "I don't want to do this," she just about whispers.

"We need to talk about it." I don't look away from her eyes, but she turns her gaze toward the door. "What are you so scared of?" I squeeze her hand.

"If we talk about this, it's going to change things. I like where we are." She turns back to look at me, and though it's not visible on the outside, I see the cracked shell her ex and her parents have left her with just below the surface.

"I like where we are too, but we can't pretend that something didn't change. I just want to talk about it. Trust me, it's not like I've figured out exactly what it means either."

Before she can respond, the chime on our phones goes off and alerts us that someone is at the front door. The relief on her face about the interruption worries me.

"I guess I should get that." I stand and point at her. "But we're not done with this conversation."

She nods somewhat solemnly, and I leave the room, jogging down the stairs to beat Theo. The bell rings again before I reach the door. I glance out the side panel and see Hannah standing there.

What the hell?

I swing the door open, my stomach bottoming out. It's not that I'm unhappy to see her—I'm happy for my son that his mother is here when he's been missing her so much.

"What are you doing here?" My words probably sound more accusing than they should, but I'm in shock.

She steps inside. "I couldn't stand being away any longer. I was already missing Theo so much, but after what happened on his birthday, I knew that was it for me." Hannah wraps me in a hug. "I was so miserable being away from him for that long. I'm never doing it again."

I hug her back because she's clearly emotional. I look over Hannah's shoulder and see Violet standing at the far end of the hallway staring at us, so I push her back. Violet dashes into the family room. Hannah's eyebrows draw together.

"Why didn't you tell me you were coming home?" I ask.

"I didn't want to say anything in case I wasn't able to get out of my contract. I couldn't stand the thought of disappointing Theo if it meant I couldn't come home early."

That makes sense. Still, she could have called me.

"Right. Well, I know he'll be excited to see you."

She smiles. "I just dropped my bags at my place and came straight here. I thought it would be fun to surprise him."

"Mommy!"

Violet must have alerted Theo to Hannah's presence because he runs out of the family room. When he reaches her, she picks him up, and he wraps himself around her. Hannah's crying into his shoulder, telling him how much she missed him, and Theo cries too. I watch as Violet awkwardly makes her way toward us. Our eyes catch for a moment, but she looks away.

"I'm so happy I'm home." Hannah bends down and sets Theo on his feet. It's then she notices Violet standing off to the side. "Violet, hi! Thank you so much for taking such great care of Theo while I was gone. I couldn't stand to be away from him any longer, so I came home early."

"Welcome home." She gives Hannah an awkward smile and wave.

Hannah, probably thinking her reaction is for reasons other than what's really going on, says, "Don't worry, we'll figure out your pay. We're not going to stiff you on what you're owed for the term of the contract just because I came home early. You'll be taken care of." She looks to me for agreement and I shift my weight.

"Yeah, of course." I clear my throat, feeling like a total douchebag.

Violet looks between the three of us, then says to Hannah, "I'll leave you three to catch up. We can figure out the details of my employment after." She walks away, not sparing us another glance.

My heart sinks to my stomach, imploring me to go after her, but I can't out us to Hannah until I know for sure what's going on.

One thing is for sure—with Hannah's return, we have no choice but to have the conversation we've been avoiding.

thirty-nine

· · ·

Violet

My emotions when I saw Hannah standing at the front door with her arms wrapped around Brady were mixed. There was definitely a note of jealousy from seeing the bond between the two of them. I was relieved because I knew how much her being home would mean to Theo, and I was devastated because it meant the end of whatever Brady and I shared.

Yes, it's clear that maybe something more can come from Brady's and my relationship. I'm really not sure since we haven't gotten to have that conversation, thanks in part to my stalling.

But I meant what I told Brady—I don't want things to change, even though they so obviously have. But now they're being forced to change again. I thought we'd have more time to figure things out and see possibilities.

I lie on my bed for a few minutes, fighting tears, feeling like my emotions are swimming through shark-infested waters and at risk of being shredded any minute.

"No, I have to do something," I murmur.

I get up off the bed and pull my clothes out from the drawers. It's clear that I'm not needed here anymore with

Hannah home. Might as well get a jump start on the inevitable.

That's how Brady finds me fifteen minutes later—shoving my clothes into my suitcase on the bed.

"What are you doing?"

I whip around, startled. "I'm packing." What else is there to say?

He walks into the room, closing the door. When I go to set a pile of clothes inside my suitcase, he closes the lid. "What the fuck, Violet? You're going to take off just like that? No conversation or anything?"

There's real pain in his eyes when I look at him, and I set down the clothes in my hands on top of the suitcase. "Hannah's home now. You don't need me anymore."

"But you're just bolting? First opportunity you have, and you're out of here rather than having a difficult conversation with me?"

It's funny when you think of a big football player and assume they wouldn't show emotions like everyone else. But Brady... Brady wears his out in the open. I'm the scared cat in the corner, clawing at anyone who comes near me.

"One has nothing to do with the other. No matter what we decide about us, I have to leave this house."

"That's not true." His hands fist at his sides.

"What are you going to do, Brady? Ask me to move in with you? That's crazy." A caustic laugh leaves my mouth.

He looks as if he wants to argue with me, but he knows I'm right. Maybe we're not in fling territory anymore, but we're not in serious territory either. We're somewhere in the middle. Maybe if Hannah hadn't come home early, we could have had the time to figure out what side of the line we fall on, but now we're out of time.

"Still, we need to have a conversation before you take off."

"Fine!" I throw my hands in the air and flop down on the bed. "Let's talk."

His forehead wrinkles and he steps toward me. "First off, what are you so pissed about?"

"Everything! Nothing! I don't even know. I think I'm a little pissed at myself for letting myself get in this situation again."

"What situation?"

He really hasn't figured it out.

"Caring for someone again." My voice is small, and I look at my hands in my lap.

"Some people might think that's a good thing." His voice grows calmer now and the bed dips beside me when he sits.

"Those people wouldn't have my history."

He takes my chin, turning it so I'm looking at him. "Just because you were with one guy who didn't know what he had doesn't mean every guy is like that."

Tears gather in the corners of my eyes, and I fight not to release them. "I was with a man for *years*, and I didn't even really know him."

He shakes his head. "I'm not him."

I know he's not. He's better than any man I've ever known and that's what makes this so scary. Can he possibly be real? If we take whatever we have and move it to the real world rather than remaining in this bubble we've created for ourselves, can it last?

"Every man I've ever thought I knew and cared about has disappointed me. Broke my heart. How do I know you're not just the next in line?" I blink and a lone tear tracks down my cheek.

"What are you talking about?" he whispers, using his thumb to brush away my tear.

I guess it's time for it all to come out. Might as well confess to him all the ugly details. Maybe then he'll understand why I can't do this. "I told you that my first job as a nanny was in college."

He nods, concern etching lines on his forehead.

"What I didn't tell you was that I worked for a single dad. He was separated from his wife and they shared custody, so I was at his place on his days with his child whenever he was at work." I swallow past the lump in my throat and force myself to continue.

"I wasn't there very long before I got the sense that he was attracted to me. He was about a decade older than me, handsome, successful in his field, and so when he paid me attention, I lapped it up. One thing led to another, and we ended up messing around whenever I was over there. He told me that he and his estranged wife had been separated for some time and were actively working on the divorce filing and had no plans to get back together. Imagine my surprise when I heard from the agency that my services were no longer needed because they'd gotten back together and she'd be moving back in."

Brady reaches for my hand, but I tug it away. I don't deserve for him to console me. "It's not your fault. He was older. He knew what he was doing."

I nod. "I know that now. I recognize that I was a naive college girl with stars in her eyes who thought she was in love, and he took advantage of that. But the fact remains that it hurt me deeply. And then when I was finally over it enough to start dating my ex, well…"

This time Brady forcibly takes my hand. "But that's not us."

I shake my head. "Everyone thinks they're the exception to the rule. Besides, do you even really know what you want? Can you honestly say you have a clear vision for the path forward for us?"

It's his split second of hesitation that seals it for me. "I know—"

I raise my hand. "You don't. And that's okay. I'm not angry. We didn't expect to have to decide this fast. It was fun while it lasted, but our time together is done."

My fight-or-flight response has kicked in, and I'm firmly in flight mode. Because when I ask myself if I'm ready to trust another man with my whole heart—and Brady would demand no less—I'm not. Especially when the man in question means so much more to me than my ex ever did. That's terrifying to think of.

Hannah's return is a good reminder that even though it may have felt like it for a short period of time, I'm not a part of this family.

"This is bullshit. You're just giving up and taking off without even trying. Without having a real conversation about how you're feeling." He stands from the bed, staring at me in anger.

"We're having that conversation right now. You just don't want to hear what I have to say."

His nostrils flare and his hands fist at his sides. "You're not really being honest with yourself right now and you know it. You had your mind made up before I came in here. You didn't even hear what I had to say."

I stand too, anger getting the better of me. "It doesn't matter. We agreed what this was at the beginning. Neither of us is ready to take it to the next level, so it's over. Let's just leave it at that."

"So you're content to bounce on Theo too? You have no issue walking away from him?" His voice shakes.

His words are like a lance to my heart. "We all knew I'd be leaving when Hannah returned." Somehow I manage to keep my voice even.

Brady shakes his head, an expression of pure disgust on his face that cuts me down until I feel five inches tall. "Fine. Have it how you want it. Congratulations, you've avoided your own possibility of heartache, but you've probably broken mine and Theo's hearts in exchange."

He stalks from the room and I crumple to the floor in silent tears so he doesn't know how devastated I am.

forty

. . .

Brady

After I leave Violet's room, it takes me a minute at the bottom of the stairs to compose myself before I join Hannah and Theo in the family room.

"Everything all right? You were gone for a while." Hannah's eyeballing me with concern.

I told her I was going to make sure Violet wasn't upset and knew that her pay wasn't in jeopardy of being cut.

I clear my throat. "Yep, all good." Then I muster up a half-ass smile to appease her.

She nods and goes back to what she's doing with Theo and his Lego set. I shouldn't be surprised that's the first place he took her. He was so excited to show her all the things he'd put together in her absence.

They do their thing for a bit while I sit quietly on the couch, going over my conversation with Violet. I can't believe she's just running away. I really didn't think this would be the outcome, regardless of how it turned out between us. But fuck it, if she wants to bolt, let her. I'm not going to beg her to stay.

Seconds after I have that thought, I hear her coming down the stairs, dragging her suitcase. I should probably go help her with the heavy bag, but I don't have it in me to look at her any more than I already have to.

She enters the family room, and I stand from the couch to say goodbye, ready to put on a show since Hannah's present. It's obvious that Violet's been crying—her eyes are red and puffy. The sight guts me, but I remind myself that she only has herself to blame for those tears.

Theo rushes over, stopping halfway when he notices the suitcase behind her. "Where are you going?"

She gets down on her knees and holds her arms out to him. "I have to go home now. Your mommy is home, so my job is over."

He rushes to her and wraps his arms around her neck. "But I don't want you to go."

I can tell from his voice that he's close to crying, and I look away and swallow hard. I catch Hannah's eye when I do, and her eyes narrow as if she senses something.

"I know. Me either, buddy. But listen..." She pulls back and sets her hands on his shoulder. "If you ever want to talk to me, your mom and your dad both have my number. You can call me anytime, okay?"

He nods and sniffles.

"It's been so wonderful getting to know you, Theo. You're an amazing boy." Violet draws him into another hug and she squeezes her eyes closed, tears running down her cheeks.

I swallow past a painful lump in my throat and my bottom lip quivers as I try to keep everything I'm feeling inside.

Violet backs away and wipes her tears as she stands.

Hannah approaches her. "Thanks again, Violet. Brady and Theo both said how amazing you were with him. I couldn't have asked for a better person to step into my role while I was away."

Violet gives her a small smile. "It was my pleasure."

"And I meant what I said about your contract. Don't

worry about the money. We'll be sure you get all you're owed."

Violet waves her off. "You don't have to do that. I'll call the agency first thing in the morning, and I'm sure they can find something for me fairly quickly. Just enjoy your time with Theo now that you're home."

Hannah pulls Violet into a hug, then everyone turns their attention to me.

My fists clench at my sides. "Thanks again." I raise one hand in a lame wave.

"No problem." Violet turns and reaches for her suitcase.

"I'll miss you," Theo calls as she leaves the room.

She stops and looks over her shoulder. "I'll miss you *too*."

The way she says too makes me think she actually meant T-W-O, but I push that thought away and turn toward Hannah and Theo. "You staying for dinner? I should probably figure something out." Anything to get the hell out of this room.

"Sure, if you don't mind," she says.

"Nope. I'm not sure if Violet already had something planned and has it out, but I'll go take a look." Without waiting for Hannah to respond, I head to the kitchen, pretending that the past couple of hours didn't just happen.

———

I insist on cleaning up after dinner just so I can be by myself under the guise of letting Hannah help Theo pack up anything he wants to take to her place for the night. She asked me if I minded and of course I don't. She's been gone a while.

I'm coming out of the pantry when the two of them appear in the kitchen, Theo with his little overnight backpack on. It seems so long since he's been gone for a night.

"Daddy, are you looking for something again?" Theo asks, head tilted.

"Just putting away something I used for dinner." I manage a smile.

Theo looks up at Hannah. "Daddy and Violet were always in there." He says it so innocently, as if he didn't just drop a bomb.

Hannah turns and looks at me. "Is that so?"

"Yep! Can we go now?" Theo jumps in place.

Hannah sets her hand on his head. "Why don't you go get your shoes on and I'll meet you at the front door? See if you can find your sandals too because we can go to the splash pad you like tomorrow."

"Yay!" Theo rushes off, hands in the air.

Hannah turns her attention back to me, eyes narrowed. "I can't believe you."

"What?" I feign innocence, walk back to the island, and pick up the cloth to wipe the counters.

"You slept with her. You slept with Violet," she says through clenched teeth.

I drop the washcloth in the sink and lean both hands on the counter. "You wouldn't get it."

"What wouldn't I get? That she's an attractive woman who's been living under your roof and *works* for you?"

"You're making it sound like something it's not."

She crosses her arms and cocks out a hip. "And what's that? That you couldn't keep it in your pants for the sake of your son? That you had to get your dick wet by fucking the nanny?"

Anger lights a torch in my chest. There have been very few times I've been angry with Hannah over the years, but right now it feels as if I could breathe fire. "You don't know what you're talking about."

"Then why don't you explain it to me? I knew something

was off when she left. That poor girl was heartbroken, and it's not just because she had to say goodbye to Theo."

I stare at her, breathing deeply and trying to calm myself before I answer.

"I met Violet six months before she started here. We slept together one night and she wouldn't give me her information, so I went back to where we met a bunch of times, hoping I'd run into her, only I didn't. The next time I saw her was when you introduced her as Theo's nanny." It's out and I feel fucking fantastic that it is.

Her forehead wrinkles. "Why wouldn't you have said something to me then?"

"Days before you were due to leave? I didn't wanna mess up the opportunity for you after you've been so supportive of my career, and if you thought she was the best one for the job, I trust your judgment. Plus, if I'm honest, I was glad to see her again. I didn't plan for anything to happen, but I'd be lying if I said a part of me wasn't excited she was back in my life."

"That still doesn't explain how you ended up sleeping with her." She puts her hands on her hips.

I roll my eyes. "We're adults. Things happen, Han."

"Like sex in the pantry when our son is in the house?"

"We were both still attracted to each other, but we agreed that Theo could never know and it wasn't supposed to be serious. It was fun, blow off some steam, and we'd both move on once her time here was done."

"How'd that work out for you? The woman who left here was not a woman who was ready to move on."

I laugh and shake my head.

"Mommy, are you coming?" Theo shouts from the front door.

"You've got it backward. She broke my heart." I push off the counter, feeling a tiny bit of satisfaction at Hannah's gaping jaw. Having been with me herself, she probably never thought it possible that I'd let a woman get close enough to affect me this much. "Let me know when you're bringing Theo home tomorrow and I'll make sure I'm around."

I leave the kitchen without a backward glance and head down to the gym, needing to get out of my head. The wound Violet's opened with her abrupt departure is an old one that will never heal—not fully at least.

forty-one

. . .

Violet

It's been just over a week since I left Brady's house in tears. Every time I feel sorry for myself, I remind myself how much worse I would feel if I'd stayed and we'd tried to make it work then broke up years later. How much more I would have been invested.

Saying goodbye to Theo broke me. I miss him as much as I miss Brady, but while it took me six months of wallowing to come out of my haze of grief before, I refuse to dive into that same hole this time. After all, I did all this so that I wouldn't end up as broken as I was after I ended my engagement.

Which is why I'm going out with Shayna and Bryce tonight. Shayna texted me a bunch of times after she caught word that Hannah was back in town and I'd moved out of Brady's house. I don't know what she knows, but I didn't want to see her at first.

She has a connection to Brady's team, so I refused her invitations the first couple of times, but since I've decided I cannot be the same woman I was after my ex-fiancé broke me, I accepted when she reached out earlier today. Besides, this could be the last time I have a chance to see her and Bryce for a while.

That doesn't mean I'm looking forward to rehashing it though. I had my fill of that when Amara stopped by my parents' earlier this week.

Still, I go through the motions, picking out a pair of black satin pants and a white flowing blouse and putting waves in my hair. It's not my usual getup for a night out, but it's the best I can do tonight. I keep my makeup minimal because I'm afraid I might cry it off anyway, and the only thing worse than crying in public is that coupled with raccoon eyes.

Once I'm ready, I head upstairs from my bedroom in the basement to leave. I hear someone shuffling around in the kitchen, so I head there to say goodbye to whoever it is. My mom is unloading the dishwasher.

"Hey, Umma." I set my purse on the counter. "I'm heading out and just wanted to say bye."

She straightens from where she is bent over the dishwasher and glances at the microwave. "So late?"

"I'm twenty-eight, Umma. Twenty-eight-year-olds can leave at nine thirty for drinks." I try to keep the snip from my voice but don't manage.

She grumbles something I can't make out, grabs some of the cutlery from the dishwasher, and walks over to the drawer to sort it. "Did your brother send you a picture of the ring yet? It's so beautiful."

My jaw clenches briefly, but I inhale a deep breath to try to relax. Being back at home has not made it any easier. Every word out of my mom's mouth is a direct dig at me. "He did. It's lovely. But then why wouldn't it be? Eric can do no wrong, right?"

She shuts the drawer and faces me, forehead wrinkled. "What's that mean?"

I guffaw. "Like you don't know. You guys think Eric walks on water. He can do no wrong while everything I do is wrong in your eyes."

I hold my breath when the words are out of my mouth.

I've never said anything like that to either of my parents and I have no idea how she'll react.

"That's not true."

Her response only further fuels my anger. "It is so. You're always disappointed in me—when I didn't win the spelling bee in fifth grade, when I didn't get valedictorian for my class like Eric did, when I left law school, when I left my cheating fiancé... should I go on?"

"We just want what's best for you." She comes to stand on the other side of the counter from me.

"I believed that. At first. But cutting me down because I can't achieve perfection just makes me feel like I'm never going to be good enough. Why won't you trust me to decide what's best for my life?"

She's quiet for a moment, and to my surprise, tears fill her eyes. "I worry for you. I only ever wanted you to be happy."

I sigh and take her hand. "Then sometimes you need to trust me. I won't always get it right, but I need to be able to make my own mistakes and not feel like you're going to be disappointed in me."

She sighs. "It's hard when you're a parent and you have to watch your child go down a path you don't think is right for them. Someday you'll see."

I squeeze her hand and let it go. I think this is the best I'll probably get from my mom, and though it's not entirely what I'd like to hear from her, I'll take it. I feel better having said something when I was too scared to for years. At least she knows how I feel now.

"I'm going to get going."

She nods. "You look very beautiful tonight. Have fun."

I smile at the rare compliment. Maybe she is trying.

It takes ten minutes to drive to the restaurant where we're having drinks. Thankfully, Shayna and Bryce agreed to come out to Santa Clara to see me so I don't have to drive into the city.

The moment I walk in and see them already waiting at a table for me, I feel like bursting into tears, but I suck them back. They stand as I approach the table, and Shayna draws me into a hug.

"How are you?" she asks when she pulls away.

Bryce steps in and squeezes me tight. "Say the word, and I'll neuter him." She's definitely the kind of girl you call when you need someone to help you bury the body.

"Hey, guys." My voice is sad as I sit across from them.

The waiter arrives to take our drink orders, and they order wine spritzers while I opt for a martini.

"You drink up. We're going to have just a little to drink so we can drive your car home for you if need be," Shayna says.

"You guys are the best." I smile and set my purse on the empty chair beside me.

Bryce doesn't wait to get into the real issue. "Now tell us everything."

"Well, what do you know?" I ask Shayna because if anyone knows anything, it will be her, though I have no idea whether Brady even told Lee what went down.

She shakes her head. "Not much. Brady told the guys that you'd left, but he didn't give any details. Said he didn't want to talk about it."

I nod. The feeling is mutual, but I won't leave these girls hanging. "You know that Hannah arrived home early unexpectedly?"

Both women nod, so I explain the series of events that led to our argument and my packing up and leaving. I tell them I don't think I'm ready to take another risk in a relationship and how I'm not sure Brady was either. I even tell them about what happened in college with the supposedly single father I was working for.

The waiter brings our drinks halfway through my story, and I take a big sip of my martini, enjoying the burn as it works its way down my throat.

When I'm done, they both sit there for a beat, collecting their thoughts.

Bryce speaks first. "It goes without saying that I want the name of that douchebag dad from when you were in college so that I can cyberstalk him and make his life miserable."

Shayna and I laugh and it goes a long way toward lightening the mood.

"How are you feeling about things now that some time has passed?" Shayna asks.

"Good question. I don't know really. He hasn't tried to contact me, so I guess that's my answer. He wasn't ready for anything serious either, so there's nothing for me to even consider. I don't know if I could take that leap of faith if he asked me, but he's not asking." I shrug with a nonchalance I don't feel. "What I know is that we couldn't go on pretending it was just a casual fling anymore."

"It's a shit or get off the pot moment, and Brady is constipated," Bryce says.

Shayna playfully smacks her arm. "Stop!"

"What? It's true." She shrugs and brings her drink to her lips.

"How is he?" I ask Shayna, looking at her from under my eyebrows.

She frowns. "Miserable. Not focused. A bear to be around."

If I thought knowing that he's suffering too would bring me any sort of pleasure, it doesn't. I nod slowly.

"If you're both miserable, maybe you should have another conversation and see what will come of it?" Shayne tilts her head and gives me a hopeful expression.

"It may not matter what I want anyway." I lift my martini glass to my lips and take a healthy sip.

"What do you mean?" Bryce asks.

"The agency received another job offer for me. They've asked if I'd be willing to relocate to Florida. They have an agency on the East Coast." I can't manage to inject any enthusiasm into my voice.

"Florida?" Shayna says in a panicked voice.

I nod. "They have a player on the Florida Fury hockey team who needs someone. I don't know exactly who—they don't tell you that until you have the job—but I guess my work with Theo and the glowing recommendation Hannah gave after I left helped get me the offer."

"Are you going to take it?" Shayna lifts her wine spritzer to her mouth and gulps down a bunch.

I shrug. "I really don't know. Part of me thinks it would be good to get away from here for a while. Clear my head, be in an environment that doesn't remind me so much of Brady. I mean, I pass that damn stadium every day. The billboards with his damn cocky smirk. Not to mention the jerseys. Seriously, how many men and boys and women wear his number with his name on it? I can't go five feet on a game day without seeing one."

Both women cringe.

"I'm not sure what I'm going to do, but I'm considering it," I say.

Bryce's shoulders sink. "When do you have to decide?"

"I have a week to figure it out, then they need to move on to someone else."

"Damn," Bryce says.

"Pretty much." I give them a sarcastic smile.

"I still think you should talk to him again," Shayna says. "He's clearly not happy without you."

"Well, he's not miserable enough to reach out to me. And anyway, I don't think he's ready for a serious relationship and all that would mean when it comes to Theo. I'm not ready to take the risk of being his guinea pig since he's never had a serious relationship since having Theo. It is what it is." Bryce opens her mouth to say something, but I raise my hand. "Can we change the topic? I know you guys mean well, but if this is my last night out with you ladies for a while, I'd really rather hear all about the amazing things going on in your lives."

They both look disappointed and like they want to say more, but Shayna nods and tells me that she and Lee are starting to talk about when they should have the wedding. Then Bryce tells us all about the horrible date she went on the night before. After a while, I almost push all thoughts of Brady and Theo to the back of my mind.

Well... almost, but not quite.

forty-two

. . .

Brady

I t's been almost two weeks since Violet walked out on Theo and me, and it doesn't hurt any less. Theo asks about her all the time, and Hannah told me that he asked her to call Violet a couple of days ago when he stayed at her place. Apparently he asked her to come to our first game of the season, which is tomorrow, and she politely declined.

Not that I expected anything different. Violet had no problem walking out on us, so why would she circle back around?

My dad texted me that he wanted to see me, so I'm heading over to his place just after lunch before Hannah is due to drop Theo off at my place. He'll be coming with me to the game tomorrow and will sit in the owner's box with my parents.

I walk into my parents' home and call out a hello, but no one answers. Evan and Bianca have returned to their respective cities on the East Coast, so it's quieter than it has been the past couple of months. It reminds me of my own house after Violet left.

Knowing my dad is likely in his office, I head over to the

stairs and make my way up there. The door is open when I reach it, so I knock lightly on the doorframe and walk inside.

"Hey, Dad. What's up?"

He looks away from his computer screen and smiles. "Thanks for swinging by." Then he stands from his desk and motions to the couch. "Have a seat."

I take a seat in the middle. "Is this about the opening game tomorrow?"

He sits in the chair to my right. "Not directly, no." He leans forward, resting his elbows on his knees. "I wanted to talk to you about Violet."

I bolt up from the couch.

"Sit down, Brady." He uses his dad voice, and even though I'm a thirty-two-year-old man, it still works on me, so I sit back down.

"I don't want to talk about it." That's what I've told anyone who's asked about it these past couple weeks.

The guys know the basics, as do my parents, but I haven't gotten into the specifics or how I'm feeling about it. I suspect my moping around gives them a pretty big clue though.

"I know you don't, but you need to. And I'm the right person to have this conversation with you. It's been weeks, and you haven't snapped out of this funk you're in, which tells me you really care for this woman."

I mimic his position and stare down through the center of my legs, admitting to my dad what I've only recently admitted to myself. "I think I love her, Dad. I didn't want to, I didn't plan on it, but there you go."

I hear his sigh. "You think or you do? Those are two very different things, Brady."

I sigh and nod. "I do."

"Brady, when I met your mom, do you think it was all sunshine and roses at first?"

I look up from the floor at him and shrug. "I don't know.

Wasn't it? All I've ever known is you guys being all about each other."

He chuckles. "True enough. But remember, I was an investment broker, and she was my best friend's little sister who wanted me to invest in a sex toy company. Does that sound like a match made in heaven?"

I laugh because, as opposite as they are, they're also so perfect for one another.

"Do you know that I didn't even tell her about you when we first met and started dating? Do you remember when we picked you up from that summer camp when you broke your arm?"

I remember seeing pictures of me with a broken arm, but not too many of the details from that day. "Sort of…"

"Hours before that was the first time she even knew you existed, and that was only because we were on a romantic weekend together and the camp called to tell me what happened."

I frown. "Why did you keep me a secret?"

He straightens up and leans back in the chair. "For the same reason you've always been so wary about women where Theo is concerned… my son's best interests were my first priority. I was wary about bringing someone into your life for years, and when Lennon came along… I felt different with her than with anyone else. But you were my priority, so I remained wary. I wanted to make sure she would be committed to me, to you, to us, but then life happened."

I nod. "That was a big part of why we agreed to keep it a secret. I didn't want Theo to be confused about what was going on." I push a hand through my hair.

"And that's what makes you an amazing father. Honestly, I couldn't be prouder of the way you're raising Theo and the way you co-parent with Hannah. A lot of people could take lessons from you two. But have you considered the fact that maybe you're doing your son a disservice by not taking a chance with Violet?"

My forehead wrinkles. "What do you mean?"

"My grandson loves that woman. I saw how they were with each other."

"So?"

He leans in. "You love that woman. Why are you denying the both of you a chance at a happy life with her?"

I stand from the couch, walk around the coffee table, and pace. "I look at how amazing Violet was with Theo, and I want her to be a part of his life. But then I feel guilty because Theo has a mother, and Hannah's a wonderful mom to him. I'm not trying to replace her, but… I don't know. It's complicated."

My dad watches me pace across his office. "There's no downfall to Theo having an abundance of people who love and care for him in his life. You know that, son, so what's this really about?"

I stop and stare at him. He always did know me best.

And so I voice my deepest, darkest fear for my son and myself. "What if things get hard and she bolts? She's already dodging conversations. She has some wounds from past relationships, and I'm not sure they've healed fully."

My dad's shoulders fall, and he walks toward me. "Brady, just because your biological mom left you doesn't mean Violet will." He brings his hands to my shoulders and looks me straight in the eyes. "Jesus, I could kill that fucking woman for abandoning you the way she did. If we didn't end up with your mom, who knows where the hell we'd be. But you know firsthand what an amazing addition a stepmother can be to a family. If Violet has issues, maybe she just needs some reassurance, maybe someone to fight for her."

I swallow past the hard, painful lump in my throat. "I don't think I could handle it, Dad. And the idea of watching Theo deal with the loss of someone he looks at as a mother figure…" I shake my head, unable to even finish that thought or put the feeling into words.

"I know, son. Believe me, I know. But if you love this woman, after all these years of you not having deep feelings for anyone, I trust that she's the right one for you. You wouldn't give your love away to just anyone. And I think your son would benefit from seeing you in a happy, committed relationship the same way you did with me."

Everything he's saying makes sense, I know it does when he explains it like this. Still, the fear of the unknown is there, looming like a dark cloud.

"Just imagine if I'd never given Lennon a chance. Where would you have gotten all your sex ed from growing up?" We both chuckle, and my dad brings his palm to my face, lightly tapping me there. "I love you, son. You deserve to be happy."

"I know, Dad. Thanks for the talk."

He pulls me in for a hug, and tears build in my eyes as I smack him on the back then pull away. I sure lucked out in the dad department.

My dad claps my shoulder and squeezes. "Give it some thought, all right?" He arches an eyebrow.

I nod. "I will."

"Good. Now go home, clear your mind, and get some rest before the big game tomorrow. This is my first in-season game as owner and you guys have to win." He winks at me.

"Yeah, yeah." I shake my head as I make my way toward the door but turn around before I leave. "Thanks, Dad. For everything."

Tears glisten in his eyes and he nods, then swallows hard before he answers. "Anything for you."

I leave with a lot on my mind, but feeling as if I have a better chance than ever at sorting out my feelings.

———

The next morning, I wake with a clear head. I know what I have to do. I have to win Violet back.

My dad was right yesterday, and when he put it in the context of his relationship with Lennon, and I started thinking about it, I couldn't believe I didn't see it for myself. My life would be so much less without Lennon in it, and I wouldn't give my love to a woman who would just up and abandon Theo and me. There's no guarantee that things will work out between us, but even if they don't, I know Violet would keep Theo's best interests at heart.

And so I'm determined to win her back and start our lives together. Right after I win this football game today.

The guys and I are in the locker room before the game and I've clued them in on what I need to do. Just like how we did when Lee fucked up with Shayna, we're all trying to figure out a plan for me to convince Violet to give us a chance, no matter how scared she is.

Miles tosses me the ball. "My mom and sister say you have to grovel. So you need to add that into your plan."

"Grovel?" Chase asks, adjusting his jock.

Miles looks at him as though he's an idiot. "You know, where you admit how you messed up and promise never to do it again and tell her how pretty and smart she is. I don't know, I've never had to do it myself."

"I want to see Chase grovel," Darius, one of the team's defensive ends, says as he walks past.

We all laugh because that would be a sight to see. Chase grumbles something under his breath.

I toss the ball to Lee. "I know what I want to say. I've got that part down. But how do I do it? I mean, do I just show up at her place with flowers or something?"

Lee shakes his head. "It needs to be bigger than that."

I grip my hair in my hand. "I'm at a loss. She's not the kind of woman who's into money, so I can't just spend a bunch on a nice present for her or something."

"Okay if I come in?" Shayna shouts from just beyond the turn into the locker room.

Lee tosses the ball back to me and looks around to make sure no one is undressed. "C'mon in, baby!"

She comes in wearing her Kingsmen football uniform and beelines it over to Lee. "Hey, guys, sorry to interrupt. I'll be quick. I just wanted to give you this." She bends at the waist and places a chaste kiss on his lips. "For good luck."

Lee grins. "Get used to it, fellas. This is our new tradition this year. I need a good luck kiss from my girl for an injury-free season."

"Can I get one of those too?" Darius shouts.

Everyone laughs and goes back to what they were doing.

"Babe, help us decide what grand gesture Brady can do to get Violet back," Lee says, tugging her into his side.

She looks from him to me, her smile dropping. She knows something.

"What?" I ask.

"Violet was offered another job… in Florida. I'm pretty sure she's taking it."

My stomach lurches. "Florida?"

Shayna nods and looks at Lee.

"When does she have to leave?"

She thinks about it, seeming to do some calculations in her head. "My guess is any day now."

"Fuck!" The ball drops from my hand and falls to the floor. "I can't leave before the game." I pace, and Chase and Miles continue to throw the football back and forth, saying the first who hits me loses. "If you fuckers hit me, you're going down."

I stop before the ball whizzes by me to Chase, and I give Shayna a pleading look. She has to have a solution. Then I go back to pacing.

Shayna steps forward. "I have an idea. What if I can get

her here before the game? You can't leave, but she doesn't live far from here... assuming she's still in town."

I'm nodding before she's even finished. "Yes, do that. I don't care what it takes, you get her here."

Fuck the grand gesture. I guess my words and my love for her will have to be enough.

Just like everything else in my life, Miles whips the ball and it hits my temple. "Motherfucker!"

They all laugh. "Just be happy it isn't Burrows who threw it, then we'd be screwed for the game."

I can't think about the game. All I can think about is, *Is Violet in sunny Florida right now?* I feel like my body should have alerted me if the love of my life was miles away.

forty-three

. . .

Violet

I'm rushing through the security of the Kingsmen stadium. When I saw Shayna's text that Brady had been hurt before the game and that Theo was upset and asking for me, I dropped everything and rushed over.

An older man escorts me through the underground of the stadium. We take a bunch of turns and I have no idea where we are, but I can tell that this area is off-limits to the public because it's all men in suits or people in uniforms with lanyards identifying themselves.

Eventually we come to the entrance to a hallway, and Shayna is there. I abandon the man with me and rush over. "Where's Theo?"

She takes a big breath and, with a worried expression, says, "Come." I walk with her until she stops again and takes both my hands. "Don't hate me."

"Violet."

I close my eyes at the sound of my name on his lips. I've longed to hear it for two weeks. Slowly, I turn around to see Brady near the end of the short hallway, dressed in his Kingsmen uniform but without a helmet on.

"Are you hurt?" I ask.

He shakes his head.

"Then bye." I spin on my heel to take off.

I can't believe Shayna got me here under false pretenses. I suppose I should've wondered why Theo was asking for me and not his mother, but all I could picture was how upset he must be and I wanted to be here to console him.

"Violet, wait."

I stop with my back turned to him.

"Can we talk since you're here? Just give me five minutes, then if you don't want to see me ever again, I'll respect your wishes."

My shoulders slump. This is why I didn't want to see him because I knew if I did, I'd be weak. I turn back around to face Brady. "You have five minutes."

He wastes no time stepping forward and taking my hand, pulling me down to the end of the hallway. This touch from him is more than I've had in weeks, and my body relishes the feel of his skin against mine.

"First, please don't be mad at Shayna. I begged her to get you here any way she could."

"Why? Why now? Don't you have a game to play?" I gesture toward his uniform.

"This couldn't wait. Shayna told me you were offered a job in Florida and that you were thinking of accepting."

He waits for me to confirm. I cross my arms and nod.

This agitates him because he pushes a hand through his hair. "Don't take the job. Stay here in California and be a part of my and Theo's lives." He takes my hands again, and I don't pull away. "I've been miserable since you left. Theo talks about you all the time too and asks me why you can't come over. I don't have the heart to tell him that it's because I'm a fucking coward who was too afraid to admit when I should have that I love you."

I suck in a breath. "Brady—"

He shakes his head. "Let me finish. The day that Hannah came back, I was too afraid to tell you that I loved you and that I wanted a full-fledged relationship with you because of my own bullshit. I didn't realize how much having my mother abandon me fucked with my head until I talked to my dad. I was just using the excuse that I wanted to protect Theo to keep you at arm's length when really all I wanted, all I needed, was to bring you into the fold."

He drops my hands and cups my face with both of his hands. I'm helpless to stop him. My heart races and tears form in the corners of my eyes.

"I love you, Violet Park, and I refuse to be without you. You're the most caring, nurturing, funny, sexy, loving, smart woman I've ever met, and I'm not going to give you up without a fight. You can tell me no today, and I'll still make my intentions known. You can move to Florida, and I'll still fight for you, for us." His gaze drifts over my face as though he's trying to study my reaction.

"I didn't take the job," I mumble.

He's the first one I've told. I turned it down, and when I did, I wasn't even sure why, just that something was keeping me here and it didn't feel right to leave.

The hope that washes over his face makes my stomach feel fuzzy.

His thumb traces a path over my cheek. "I know you're scared to love again, but please give me a chance. I promise to heal those wounds of yours. I promise to show you how you should be treated and I won't stop until you believe in our happily ever after."

I am still scared. Petrified even. But my gut tells me this is right, this is where I'm supposed to be.

"I love you, Brady Banks."

His lips are on me in a second, and I melt into his kiss. For the first time in weeks, the tension leaves my body and I'm at home in my own skin. When he pulls away, he rests his forehead against mine and whispers, "I promise I'm going to make you so happy."

I almost faint when he lets go of my face and drops to one knee, reaching for my hand. "Violet, I might be pushing my luck here, and I know it's crazy, but I don't want to wait for some undetermined amount of time. You dated a guy for years and got engaged and look how that turned out. Marry me."

I yelp.

"I don't have a ring or anything because I wasn't planning on doing this today, but I'll buy you the biggest, flashiest, gaudiest ring you can find. Or a classic solitaire, which I suspect might be more your style." He winks, and I giggle like a schoolgirl.

"I want it all with you, and I'm not afraid to tell you that here today. I want to marry you and have babies with you and raise a family. One of the things I love most about you is how you are with Theo, and it would be a blessing and an honor to share children with you. And if you're not ready today, that's fine. But know this is where we're headed whenever you're ready. One day, I want you in my bed every night and in my pantry every morning."

We laugh.

I blink, and a tear drips down my face. This man is crazy. We just got back together and now he's proposing to me?

As I stand there staring at him, I wait for fear to rise up in me, but it doesn't come. In fact, the only emotion that registers right now is pure joy.

I swallow hard and squeeze his hand. "What's that saying? In for a penny, in for a pound?"

"Is that a yes?"

With tears in my eyes, I nod. "That's a yes."

He pops up off the floor and lifts me up, swinging me

around. "You've made me the happiest man in the world." When he sets me down, his lips are on mine again.

Some kind of announcement is made out on the field. I can't make out what it says, but Brady must know because he pulls away.

"C'mon. Let's go up to the owner's box and tell my family. The twins flew into today for the game since it's the first one for my parents as owners. Theo's going to be so excited." He takes my hand and starts to walk, but I drag him to a stop.

"Are you sure you want to tell everyone today?"

He scowls at me. "You thinking of changing your mind?" I shake my head. "Good. Me either. Now let's go."

Brady leads me down a few hallways and to an elevator that takes us to the boxes. We make out the entire time and almost miss getting off when it reaches our floor.

We head down the hallway hand in hand, and the fact that he's up here so close to game time seems to draw a lot of attention. Everyone who notices us murmurs to each other, watching where we're headed.

He stops in front of a door with a sign that reads Owner's Suite and opens the door. Everyone inside turns to look at us. I notice his parents smiling when they see our joined hands, but my attention is quickly diverted when Theo calls my name.

"Violet! You're back!" He runs at me from his grandpa.

I let go of Brady's hand and drop to my knees, arms wide open. Theo's little body crashes into mine and I almost fall back, but Brady's hand on my back steadies me. I squeeze Theo tightly and glance up at Brady, who's looking at us as though he's overcome with emotion.

God, I'm so happy to have these two guys back in my life. I'll never take them for granted.

Theo finally lets go of me and steps back. "I'm so happy you're here!"

"Me too, buddy." I ruffle his hair, then Brady helps me stand up.

"I have something I need to tell everyone," Brady says.

Oh man, he really isn't wasting any time with this.

"Violet has agreed to be my wife."

Cheers echo throughout the room, the loudest coming from Theo, who's jumping up and down. Then he stops and looks at us. "What?"

Brady picks him up and quickly explains how we fell in love and we're going to get married. Theo smiles and nods. "When did you fall in love?"

No one says anything.

He leans over to my parents and whispers, not too softly, "In the pantry."

Everyone laughs.

Jasper and Lennon come over to give me a hug and offer us their congratulations. If they're concerned about this whirlwind engagement, they show no signs of it.

Then Bianca hugs her older brother, then me. And finally, Evan gives me a hug.

When he pulls away, he smirks and looks at his brother. "I think you're with the wrong brother, but he's a close second." He winks, and Brady playfully punches him in the shoulder.

There's an announcement over the speaker in the stadium, and Jasper glances at the clock. "I think you have somewhere you need to be."

Brady nods and looks at me reluctantly.

"Go." I wave him off. "I'll see you after."

He kisses me, deepening it to what is more than appropriate given our audience.

"Get a room," Evan yells.

"They're in a room," Theo says, and Brady and I end the kiss laughing.

"Go out there and be a winner," Lennon shouts as Brady makes his way to the door.

He stops and turns around to look at me. "I already won today, no matter what happens out on that field."

I smile as Theo takes my hand and leads me to the windows so we can see the field. The entire game, as I watch my future husband play his heart out, all I can think of is how I belong here. And for a girl like me, that's all I've ever wanted.

epilogue

. . .

Brady

A week and a half after I asked Violet to marry me, she moved into my place with Theo and me, and things couldn't be more perfect. Some might think I'm crazy for proposing to Violet minutes after we got back together, but how's that for a grand gesture?

Let's see one of my buddies try to top that.

We've just dropped Theo off at Hannah's for the night and are headed over to Chase's for an impromptu celebration with some of the team to celebrate our engagement. Chase wasn't happy about being chosen as host, but we all agreed that since he never has us over to his place, his time is up.

We just have to make one pit stop on the way.

I turn off the route that we'd need to take to Chase's, but Violet doesn't seem to notice. As soon as I park in front of a bunch of shops where there are no condo buildings to be found, she looks at me quizzically.

"Chase lives around here?"

"Nope." I lean over and draw her in for a kiss.

She chuckles as she pulls away. "All right, what are we doing here then?"

"It's a surprise. C'mon." I get out of the car and walk

around the front to open her door and help her out. Once we're hand in hand on the sidewalk, I lead her toward our destination.

"Brady, where are we going?"

"Here." I stop us in front of the jewelry store where I picked out a ring for her two days after I proposed. I had to guess on the sizing, so I hope it fits. Violet hasn't asked once about the ring, which shouldn't be a surprise, but I want my ring on her finger. I want the entire world to know this woman is mine.

She glances at the sign and her hand flies up to her mouth. "What's going on?"

"Let's go inside and see." I hold open the door then follow her inside.

"Mr. Banks, hello again," Marcelle, the jeweler I worked with last week, says when we enter.

"Marcelle, this is my beautiful fiancée, Violet. Violet, Marcelle." I motion between the two of them.

He holds out his hand. "Pleasure to meet you. Congratulations on your engagement."

"Thank you." Violet's smile is so wide and genuine that I know I did the right thing by picking her ring out myself.

I wasn't sure whether she would want to do it, but I figured since we had a nontraditional proposal, it would be okay if I went the traditional route and chose the ring for her.

"Are you ready to get started?" Marcelle asks me.

I nod. "Please."

He reaches under the counter and brings out a maroon ring box and slowly opens it. The four-carat cushion-cut solitaire set on an eternity band sparkles under the lights.

Violet gasps. "Oh my god, Brady, it's too much." She shuts the box.

I laugh and slowly open it back up. "Nothing is too much for you. Should we see if it fits?"

Our eyes meet, and she nods. I remove the ring from the

box, take her left hand in mine, and slip the ring on her ring finger.

"It's a perfect fit," Marcelle says, sounding pleased.

"I went for something classic that's still a little flashy. Kind of like the woman wearing it."

She places her hand on my cheek and kisses me. "I love it."

"Are you sure?" I arch an eyebrow. "Because if not, you can choose whatever you like."

Violet's shaking her head before I finish speaking. "No, I want this one. You chose it."

"Do you think your mom will approve?"

We both laugh. My meeting with her parents went all right until we told them we were engaged and that she'd be moving in with me. Her parents both shouted rapid-fire Korean, none of which I understood, and I think Violet probably only told me half of everything they said. But the gist was they didn't understand how she could be engaged to a man she'd just met who was already a parent outside of marriage. And why wasn't there a ring?

So we're not off to the best start, but I have every confidence I can win them over. And if not, Violet and I will be fine either way.

"I approve, and that's all that matters." She kisses me again until Marcelle clears his throat, and we pull back from each other.

"Sorry." Violet's cheeks are red, and I chuckle.

I thank Marcelle again for his help, and we go back out to the car and drive over to Chase's building. Once we park, we head inside and check in with the concierge. Since we're on the list, he lets us through to the elevator.

I stab the button for the thirty-third floor when I hear a woman shout, "Hold the elevator, please!"

Violet presses and holds the door open button until a

woman carrying a large box steps on. It's not until she sets it down at her feet that I realize who she is.

"Twyla? I didn't know you were in town."

Her shocked gaze turns our way. "Brady? Violet? Oh my god, congratulations! My brother told me the news." She steps around the box as the elevator doors close and gives us each a hug.

"Thanks. When did you get into town?" I ask.

"I flew in yesterday."

"Oh, Miles didn't mention it."

She bites her lower lip. "He doesn't exactly know yet."

Violet's head tilts. "Are you here to surprise him?"

"No… I actually moved here. At least temporarily." She cringes.

"Oh my god, that's awesome!" Violet envelops her in another hug.

"Thanks. I'm hoping my brother will think so. I'm not sure if he'll feel like I'm cramping his style or what, but I needed to get away from the East Coast. It reminds me of how my life imploded, so I took a leave of absence from work and found a job house-sitting for some big-time tech executive who's in Asia for a few months. I always love San Francisco when I visit, so I figured, why not?" She shrugs.

"And the place you're living is in this building?" I ask.

Violet looks giddy with excitement.

"Yeah. Oh my god, I didn't even hit the button for my floor." She turns toward the panel, arm outstretched, then lets it drop. "Thirty-three. That's where I'm headed too." She turns back around to face us. "I haven't even asked… what are you guys doing here?"

"There's a get-together tonight to celebrate our engagement with some of the team. Chase has been forced to host." I can't help my snicker. "He lives on the thirty-third floor."

She smiles. "That's the same floor I'm on."

Well, this should be interesting, to say the least.

The elevator dings and the doors open.

"Here, let me get that box for you." I bend and pick it up.

"Oh thanks. It's the last of my things that I sent ahead." She leads us down the hall toward her apartment, and when we stop in front of apartment eleven, I realize her door is directly across from Chase's.

"Chase is right across the hall from you," I tell her.

"No way! It'll be nice to see a familiar face."

"Yeah, definitely. Can't wait to see how it turns out." I grin.

Violet gives me a strange look, probably wondering why the hell I'm acting so weird.

"Oh shit, is my brother in there? I don't want him to find out like this. I should—"

Chase's door whips open without warning, and I turn to see him filling the doorframe. "Thought I heard you out here. What the hell, are you trying to piss off all my—" He comes to an abrupt halt when he notices Twyla standing with us.

"Funny thing, we just met your new neighbor." When I nod toward Twyla, all the color drains from Chase's face, and he looks as if he might be sick.

Oh yeah, this is going to be *really* interesting.

The End

cockamamie unicorn ramblings

We can't tell you how thrilled we were to be able to write Brady Banks' story! He played a pivotal role in his parents' story and to write him all grown up as a father himself was so much fun to explore! (Sidenote: If you're interested in Jasper and Lennon's story you can check out *Mad About the Banker*.)

Brady was a fun character to explore. In Lee's book he came off a bit as the proverbial playboy, and he definitely was that for a period of his life. But once he met Violet he was done for, and we were happy to reunite the two. LOL What really makes Brady the perfect book boyfriend in our opinion is his relationship with Theo. That man loves his son and would do anything for him. And once he realized Violet was on his list of people he loves, there was no stopping him.

Was it a crazy decision to have Brady propose seconds after they got back together? Maybe! But it felt authentic to their characters. They're both the kind of people who once they know what they want they get after it 100%. These two are going to want to be married ASAP and start having babies.

In regard to Brady's relationship with Theo's mother, Hannah, we purposely did not want to write them as having an antagonist relationship. We felt like these were two mature characters who were able to put their differences aside and had a good amount of respect for each other as co-parents. It would have been easy to make her the evil ex, and hey, sometimes you need one of those in a story, but it just didn't feel right in this case.

Violet's relationship with her parents while not perfect had improved by the end of the story. You might notice that we do that sometimes. The couple's relationship will always be wrapped up in a pretty bow, but sometimes those outlier relationships won't have such an easy fix. We do that on purpose. Sure, this is fiction and not real life, but it's hard to try to fix decades of animosity in one conversation. But a conversation can be a starting point and that's true to life. We also love that it shows that our couple can still end up happy and fulfilled even if they don't have the control to fix *every* relationship in their life.

We have a lot of people to thank for getting this book to market:

Nina and the entire Valentine PR team.
Cassie from Joy Editing for line edits.
Ellie from My Brother's Editor for line edits.
Rosa from My Brother's Editor for proofreading.
Hang Le for the cover and branding for the entire series.
All the bloggers who read, review, share and/or promote us.
The Piper Rayne Unicorns in our Facebook group who give us a safe space online to chat and show us love on the daily!
Every reader who took a chance on this book! Thank you for granting us your most precious resource—time. We hope you felt it was well worth it.

Next up in the series is Chase and Twyla's story and boy

oh boy do we love a grumpy/sunshine, brother's best friend setup! Add on that they're now neighbors? *Chef's kiss*

We hope you're ready for more of our football players, we know we are!

xo,
Piper & Rayne

about piper & rayne

Piper Rayne is a USA Today Bestselling Author duo who write "heartwarming humor with a side of sizzle" about families, whether that be blood or found. They both have e-readers full of one-clickable books, they're married to husbands who drive them to drink, and they're both chauffeurs to their kids. Most of all, they love hot heroes and quirky heroines who make them laugh, and they hope you do, too!

also by piper rayne

On Thin Ice

Break the Ice

Box Set

Charity Case

Manic Monday

Afternoon Delight

Happy Hour

Blue Collar Brothers

Flirting with Fire

Crushing on the Cop

Engaged to the EMT

White Collar Brothers

Sexy Filthy Boss

Dirty Flirty Enemy

Wild Steamy Hook-up

The Rooftop Crew

My Bestie's Ex

A Royal Mistake

The Rival Roomies

Our Star-Crossed Kiss

The Do-Over

A Co-Workers Crush

Hockey Hotties

My Lucky #13

The Trouble with #9

Faking it with #41

Sneaking around with #34

Second Shot with #76

Offside with #55

Kingsmen Football Stars

You had your chance, Lee Burrows

You can't kiss the Nanny, Brady Banks

Over my Brother's Dead Body, Chase Andrews

The Baileys

Lessons from a One-Night Stand

Advice from a Jilted Bride

Birth of a Baby Daddy

Operation Bailey Wedding (Novella)

Falling for My Brother's Best Friend

Demise of a Self-Centered Playboy

Confessions of a Naughty Nanny

Operation Bailey Babies (Novella)

Secrets of the World's Worst Matchmaker

Winning My Best Friend's Girl

Rules for Dating your Ex

Operation Bailey Birthday (Novella)

The Greenes

My Beautiful Neighbor

My Almost Ex

My Vegas Groom

The Greene Family Summer Bash

My Sister's Flirty Friend

My Unexpected Surprise

My Famous Frenemy

The Greene Family Vacation

CPSIA information can be obtained
at www.ICGtesting.com
Printed in the USA
BVHW030408140223
658390BV00004B/131

9 798887 142173